Casey grabbed the enemy agent . . .

by the face and forced his mouth open. A gout of bright red blood gushed forth spewing across the room and covering Casey's hands.

"Goddamn it! the son of a bitch has bitten his tongue off and swallowed it!"

CASCA:

THE PHOENIX

#14

BARRY SADLER

CHARTER BOOKS, NEW YORK

CASCA #14: THE PHOENIX

A Charter Book / published by arrangement with
the author

PRINTING HISTORY
Charter edition / August 1985

ISBN: 0-441-09329-9

Charter Books are published by The Berkley Publishing Group,
200 Madison Avenue, New York, New York 10016.
PRINTED IN THE UNITED STATES OF AMERICA

Boston, Massachusetts

My dear Landries:

It has been a time since I last wrote you. I hope you have enjoyed the previous episodes of our wandering friend's experiences. He does not look well, although he is not ill. You and I both know that could not be the case. How can I put it? The man is just extraordinarily tired. A great weariness of the soul hangs upon him. There have been times for both of us when, as doctors, we have wished for the death of patients so ill that there was no hope for them except death to relieve their suffering. I often feel that for Casca. If I could I would give him that which he seeks. For surely there has never been anyone that has ever walked the face of this earth that has known such endless suffering in so many ways. But enough of that; we both know that there is nothing that either one of us can do for him. Yet I feel that somehow talking to him and sharing some of his experiences gives him a little relief.

When last we talked you asked me if I could find out what happened to him during his time in Vietnam before he was brought to us at the 8th Field Hospital in Nha Trang. Well I have just returned from another meeting with him and he had no objections. Therefore, I most humbly submit the enclosed for your approval and dissection. . . .

CHAPTER ONE

Mud, the texture and color of blood, bubbled in his mouth as his lungs tried to breath through the slimy fluid. Deep emerald-green leaves and the thick brush glistened with the pearldrops of the afternoon rain.

A foot pushed at his back, tentatively at first, then more insistent as it stomped against his spine, forcing a groan out of his chest. Through the mist of his half-conscious pain he could hear voices in Vietnamese:

"This one is alive."

Hands turned him over to his back, stripping his boots and gear from his body. His leg twisted under him at an impossible angle as the Vietcong guerrillas moved to his back. The left leg was fractured below the knee, broken by the explosion of a mine set off five feet in front of him by the point man.

Through the daze of his fogged mind he could hear single sharp cracks as brain shots were administered to each of the five already dead Americans. At the command of their leader, the VC jerked the surviving member of the patrol to his feet, supporting him so his face could be seen by their commander. A sharp slap across the face helped to bring Sgt. Casey Romain's eyes into focus. Soft brown eyes looked directly into Casey's. The once gray-blue color of his own eyes were covered by a thin film of blood caused by the concussion of the land mine. The Vietnamese officer spoke to him, his words gently flavored by the accents of France where he had been educated.

"Can you hear me?" Another slap evoked a spontaneous response from the object of the Viet officer's attention. Casey's head jerked straight up. Eyes glaring with hate, they locked on the smooth, tan, intelligent face before him.

"Good," continued the soft voice. "Good, I see you do understand me." At the Viet's side came another, harsher, voice. Casey couldn't make out the words but the tones were filled with urgency. The soft voice cut the other one short.

"Well now." He moved his eyes to examine the rank of his prisoner. "Well now, Sergeant, it seems that this is not your lucky day. My associate tells me that we have to move on rather quickly. Our scouts have spotted some of your people heading this way and we're not prepared to greet them properly. From the look of your leg it is obvious that you would only slow us down. I do wish that I had the time to visit with you in a more congenial manner. I am certain that we would find many things of mutual interest to discuss. But, as they say, War is Hell." The voice laughed easily at the joke. "Yes, war is hell so prepare for your entry."

Colonel Ho van Tuyen, of the People's Army of Liberation, was sincere in his regret that they would not have an opportunity to get to know each other better. It was always satisfying for him to reduce his captives to mindless whimpering creatures while proving his mastery over them. He sighed with regret. There were so few things that he really enjoyed, and it was difficult to pass up the opportunity to experience one of them, but then one can't have everything.

From the edge of the clearing, where the ambush had taken place, came a cry from one of his Bo Doi. "There is another one alive!"

Colonel Tuyen turned his attention to this new offering. A young trooper, not yet nineteen, was dragged before him. He, like Romain, was wounded. A red stain on his camouflage jacket and frothy bloody bubbles from the mouth were evidence enough that the young man was suffering from a shrapnel wound in his chest. He too would not be worth taking. To Romain he directed his words. "Oh yes, this is indeed an unfortunate day for you and your comrade friend here. But even though we are in a bit of a hurry I shouldn't deprive my own men of their small pleasures." He turned to his men and signaled them to begin. Five Vietcong gathered in a circle around the young trooper who was just beginning to understand what was going to happen. To him it seemed impossible that only three weeks ago he had been with his girl friend in Denver; now he was in this nightmare place and something horrible was about to happen to him. He opened his mouth for a scream that never came. The butt of an AK-47 assault rifle crushed his jaw driving broken bone splinters and teeth back into his throat. Arms raised around him as he was forced to his knees. Knives, machetes and bayonets flashed in the afternoon sun as they rose and fell. The weapons dripped with the blood of the nineteen year old as the soldiers hacked him into pieces with practiced strokes, severing his arms at the shoulder, then severing the head from the neck as he knelt in front of them.

Casey's eyes were fully focused now as he witnessed the butchering of the young man. There was nothing he could do. His good leg wouldn't even hold up his own weight. For the first time he spoke, his eyes unblinking, locked on the face of Ho van Tuyen. "You shouldn't have done that." An impulse to laugh at the American's futile remark was stifled in Ho's throat as he found his eyes forced to move away from those of his captive. He felt as if the man he was about to have killed was memorizing every feature of his face. A cold chill of fear ran through him as the light colored eyes looked at him as if he were already a dead man. His aide, Dai Uy Troung, urged him to get on with it. They had no time to waste. Ho shook off his fear. After all, he was in control here and this man would be dead in just a few seconds.

Casey knew what was going to happen. "Be seeing you around Colonel."

"*Sat Ngui My!*" The order to kill the strangely disconcerting American was obeyed instantly. But this time not with the machetes or by the quick grace of a brain shot. There was no time left for small amusements and he would do nothing to give the approaching Americans any warning. This time it was done with a single thrust of the triangular shaped bayonet attached to the muzzle of a SKS assault rifle. The point entered Casey's chest, sinking deep. The smaller Viet gave the rifle a strong solid push, forcing the point out of Casey's back near the spine. Blood filled Casey's lungs. He sucked in air then expelled it with a gush of bright red blood. When he fell it was to lie crumpled and still. Not knowing why, Ho bent over the body to inspect it, despite the urgings of Troung to leave. Ho touched the open eyes with his fingers. No response. He felt for a pulse in the carotid artery; there was none. "Good!" One last order was given. His men dragged the bodies of the dead Americans off into the brush concealing them from casual observation. Because of the presence of the enemy they had not been able to take the time to properly strip the bodies. Only weapons and ammunition were taken, much to the regret of the VC, who were very fond of American jungle boots. Satisfied at last he and his men faded wraithlike back into the relative safety of the jungle to continue their mission. The ambush of the American patrol had not been on his agenda. He had simply taken advantage of a target of opportunity. Now he had to return to his real work, the organizing of special squads whose sole purpose was to kill the brains of the opposition —including high ranking South Vietnamese and American officers as well as the politicians and other influential traitors who served the Americans in the provinces. Village chiefs, prominent businessmen and province governors were even now being marked for death—and he was the mind behind the plan which would strike them down. Before he was through, it would take either an extraordinarily brave man or a fool to accept a position of responsibility.

The clearing was left behind. Flies had started gathering on the bodies to drink the fluid which already was turning black and gummy from the heat. The blood would not fully dry for some time yet, the humidity giving it a gluelike texture until it did.

The scouts of the advancing American patrol missed the clearing where the ambush had taken place by a mere hundred meters. They had heard the distant sounds of gunfire, but because of the density of the terrain they had been unable to get a firm fix on it. They only knew that they hadn't been able to raise their missing friends on the radio. They gave the clearing a quick once over and then moved on. If they had spent a moment looking they might have noticed the dark stains on the grass or the dull glint of light reflected off the spent brass of an M-16 or AK-47. They didn't. The bodies of their friends remained where they were hidden in the brush. Only the flies and birds knew where they were.

All that day and into the night the dead lay still. Two hours before dawn one of them began to move. A finger trembled, pores opened to sweat. This body had not begun to swell with internal gas; the limbs were not bloated nor the face turning black with death. A pulse tentatively beat in the carotid artery, and then, as if gaining confidence, increased in strength and regularity. Sgt. Casey Romain, aka Casca Rufio Longinus, was coming back once more from the black depths of death, leaving behind the darkness he had wished for countless times. Damn the day he plunged his spear into the one who hung from the crucifix. Since that fateful moment he was doomed to walk the earth until the Second Coming. Only then would he finally have that which he sought most— eternal sleep. But for now, he would rise once more. And this time when he rose, it would be with a lust for vengeance.

His lungs tried to turn themselves inside out as they expelled the last of the thick blood which filled them. Finally they sucked in air to inflate the organs and pump life into the now quivering body. Tear ducts began to function, moistening the delicate tissues of the eyes, permitting them to blink once, then again. The puncture marks from the triangle shaped bayonet were already closed. Only pink puckered marks showed the entry and exit points of the blade. Pain added to his resurrection. Groaning, he pushed his way out of the tangle of limbs and bodies that covered him. His uniform was black with clotted blood and swarms of flies clung to him, sucking the blood of those who had died. But the mindless creatures somehow knew to leave his blood alone.

He staggered, and then his legs collapsed under him. The fractured bone where the 7.62 mm bullet had passed through his femur was still out of alignment though the wound itself had closed. Groaning with pain as the pieces of bone grated against each other under the weight of his body, he fell back to the earth. Eyes fogged, he blinked several times till the darkness around him began to take form. For a moment he had thought he was completely blind but it was only the night. Crawling over to where the bole of a tree split close to the ground, he set his foot between the branching trunk so that it served as a wedge. When he was ready he took a deep breath, held it, then drew his injured leg back pulling the fracture into line under the skin. He thought he could hear the squeaking of the bone being transmitted up his leg to the mastoid behind his ears. Head swimming with nausea, he waited for the pain to pass.

Tendrils of fog floated over the trees. The thin glow of a cloud-shrouded quarter moon cast its haze over the brush. He shook his head, moving away from the pile of bodies. He needed to drink. The membranes of his mouth and throat were as dry as parchment. When the worst of the pain had subsided, he began to grope his way from the ambush site, following a thin animal trail through the trees. He grew stronger with every step as his body and mind cleared itself of the experience of touching death then being drawn away from it.

Dampness soaked through the olive drab canvas sides of his jungle boots. A stream! Kneeling, he lowered his face to the liquid and drank, sucking the fluid in with huge gulps. His stomach wretched, spewing it back out, cleaning itself. Then he drank again, only this time more slowly, letting the moisture seep slowly into his dried gums and the delicate lining of his throat. The water stayed down. There by the narrow stream he rested, washing his face and rinsing as much of the blood out of his uniform as he could. He wanted a smoke. Resting his back against a smooth tree trunk, he closed his eyes, bringing to the front of his mind the face of Ho.

With every fiber of his being he summoned back the instinctive hate he had for the VC colonel although he had met him just once. The deaths of the men in his patrol and the manner in which Ho had had the young trooper butchered only added to his hate. He wasn't shocked by the deaths for in his time he had seen tens of thousands die in every conceivable manner and knew he would see even more before he was finally permitted to join their ranks. But now he had a cause, a purpose to his existence. He was going to find Ho. No matter where he was or how far he might run, Casey was going to look him in the eyes again. This was one time when the curse of Golgotha was welcome and he would use it, even if it meant he had to die a dozen times more before he at last had his strong scarred hands on the throat of the Vietnamese. He was not impatient, for he had time on his side, all the time in the world. . . .

There had been another time when he had been with the French Foreign Legion that he had been left for dead on a Vietnamese trail. He wondered if that would happen yet again before he was at last done with this ancient land of smiling graceful people and rotting death.

Enough! He had things to do before this day was through, and he couldn't get them done by sitting on his ass. There was nothing he could do for those in the clearing but there was much he could do to those that killed them. He rose to move north. The light had cleared enough for him to see spoor on the ground. The marks of many feet. The Vietcong were going north. So was he. . . .

CHAPTER TWO

Ho never gave the strange-eyed man another thought. After the incident he'd even felt a bit silly for letting his thoughts carry him away. What could he possibly have had to fear from one who had been so completely in his power and now was dead? As dead as the rest of the patrol. He had been fighting long enough to know that dead men can't hurt anyone. Two more days and they would reach their destination across the Cambodian border near where Vietnam, Laos and Cambodia touched corners. There, in a secure area, his agents and assassins, his *"Ke' sat Nhan,"* were being trained and made ready for their day of use. Ho had long been fascinated by the story of the original assassins of Hassan ibn Hassad and the effect that they'd had on the course of history. The ancient assassins of Persia were a prime example of the power of selective terrorism, demonstrating quite clearly how a few men who were willing to die, could strike blind fear and panic into the minds and hearts of the so-called upper classes, rendering them powerless despite their armies and castles. His reverie was broken by Captain Troung. He was pointing out their approach to the village of Plei Tangale. It was a small hamlet of no great importance, peopled by

members of the Bihnar tribe of Montagnards,
those aboriginal savages of the Annamite highlands who held such a strong physical resemblance
to the American Indians of the last century: wiry,
stringy-muscled, a bit taller and darker than the
Vietnamese, with long hair that hung to the
shoulders and smelled of smoke.

Of late the Vietnamese on both sides had
changed their policies concerning the natives and
had been actively courting their favor. Ho felt that
his party had the best offer to make them. If they
supported the revolution then they would be
granted an autonomous republic inside the sphere
of the new government and allowed to continue
their own way of life without any interference
from the Vietnamese. This had already been done
in North Vietnam and several influential Montagnard leaders had made the trip north and had
returned with high praise for the situation in the
Peoples Republic. Ho knew that once victory was
achieved the so-called autonomous regions would
quickly be reduced to their proper state and the
savages once more put in their place. But for now
there were several hundred thousand of them that
could be of use and put into the field, thus saving
the lives of his own men. To that end, when he saw
Moh Chen, the village chief, a dark, dry-skinned
man of middle age with wide shoulders and mus-
cular arms, wearing a loincloth and a red and
black striped native blanket of homespun cotton
approach him, he was all smiles.

His men were already in the village, trading for
food, and gathering a few chickens and some rice
for the evening pots. Ho made absolutely certain
that everything his men took was paid for and

without cheating. He needed the support of the villages in the region. Once he had them on his side they would serve as the eyes and ears that would warn him of danger long before it came too near to him. Everything was all smiles and welcome between the two men as greetings were exchanged in a mixture of Vietnamese and Bihnar. Both knew the other was not completely sincere, but the game had to be played. Ho dined somewhat unwillingly with the chief on a meal of fat roasted dog and rice served with the ever present "*nouc mam*," a fish sauce that was highly prized among the aborigines. Montagnard cuisine left much to be desired. The dog was simply gutted and tossed on a bed of coals to cook off its hide. When a portion looked done enough it was just torn off and eaten.

After dining, Ho made a few small gifts to the chief in the form of cigarettes taken from the dead Americans he'd ambushed. Then he departed leaving three men behind in the village to keep an eye on the trail and to serve as an additional incentive for the Montagnard chief to toe the line.

Casey dined on no such exotic a meal. Much of his nourishment came from a hunger to get his hands on Ho. He did eat but didn't taste the flesh of the large, slow, tree lizard that had crossed his path. Iguana was a delicacy in many parts of the world, but he had not time to think about such niceties.

The spoor was growing clearer; he was gaining on them. While the Vietcong rested in the Bihnar camp he traveled, each step bringing him that much closer to the object of his hatred, the man called Ho.

Ho had no desire to tarry in the camp of the savages. After the basic amenities had been observed, he'd felt free to continue on to the base camp in a valley branching off the Song Cai River. The presence of his three well-armed men would be more than sufficient to insure the continued loyalty of the tribe. There would be no trouble from those animals. The chief knew all too well that the less than effective security of the Saigon forces was too far away to do his people any good. To him it didn't make much difference who the masters were or what ideology they espoused. To Moh Chen they were all the same. Both sides were hated equally, for both sides were Vietnamese and had been the hereditary enemies of his race since time immemorial. He would do what he had to for the safety of his tribe. That was his only concern and if it required paying lip service to the North Vietnamese or Vietcong then so be it. He would treat the Saigon Forces no differently if they came to his village. Spears, crossbows and a few rusty Mats bolt action rifles left over from the French were no match for AK-47s or M-16s.

Troung took the position behind their point man, his mind on his leader. He had a great admiration and respect for Comrade Ho and knew that he was in a favored position. Ho's star was on the rise. If his plan for the disruption of the enemies' morale and their will to resist was successful, there was no limit to how far he could climb in the ranks of those who would rule this land when the Americans and their puppets, the South Vietnamese, were defeated. That Ho would succeed was never a matter for doubt, but he was a bit concerned about Ho's occasional irrational behavior where prisoners were concerned. Not that he found any of Ho's actions reprehensible; it was only the degree of his passion that concerned Troung. Passion was not a good thing where business was concerned; it clouded the mind and judgment. Ho was fortunate that he, Troung, was at his side to provide a cooler head when the occasional moments of passion overcame his leader. He would be glad when they were back in their camp, even though it meant a night march from the village of Plei Tangale to the far banks of the Song Chi River.

Casey watched the haze of blue smoke from the cooking fires rise over the Bihnar village. Dawn was still a couple of hours away and soon they would start to awaken. He wanted to be done and away before then. A thin-ribbed dog scratched itself with its right hind leg, thought about it for a moment then rose, stretched its back, and went to leave its scent on a nearby post used for the butchering of an occasional deer or pig. He sniffed the post before relieving the pressure in his bladder. The smell of old blood brought saliva to its jaws as it wondered when it would taste red meat again.

Sliding along a drainage ditch, Casey moved, body low to the ground, taking advantage of all cover, staying in the shelter of the mist rising from the floor of the damp lands floating over him like the spirit of the dead in the predawn hours. The coolness of the mist contrasted with the heat of his own body's furnace that was generating the feelings of hate that stayed with him. In the village he hoped to find that which he sought and needed. He knew he was close, and the fact that there were

sentries on duty was a good sign. Still, he hadn't
been able to determine in which huts the Vietnamese were sleeping. It was too dark and too far
to see. He would just have to go down and find
Comrade Ho. Somewhere in one of the huts, if he
was lucky, he'd find him and then kill him.

Pausing, he lowered his stomach to the damp
earth. A sentry walked his post, half-awake and
bored from the long night, his lids thick with the
heaviness that always came in the long hours
before the sun rose. Casey waited, patient. Give
the man time! The sentry turned his back and
began to walk to the far edge of the village where
the cooking fire was still smouldering, giving off
pungent wisps of smoke to ride with the mist.
Casey followed after him. Half crawling he closed
on his target. A pariah dog smelled him and
started to give a warning growl, then changed its
mind. This was not something it wanted part of
and the animal could smell the coming death.
Placing its tail between its legs the dog arched its
back in a sign of submission and turned away to
hide under the floor of one of the longhouses.

Rising to his feet, Casey kept to the dark shadows of the longhouses as he closed in on his prey.
He needed the man's weapons. During the time he
had been watching, the Viet sentry had made the
same pattern twice. Soon he would come back
from the east side of the village to face out to
where a small grove of plantains were nearly ready
for picking.

Doan Le Quan was not very concerned about
the presence of enemies this close to the border
and guard duty was always boring. His AK-47
hung from its shoulder strap as he made what he

thought was another endless round of the village perimeter. His thoughts were concentrated more on when his relief would come than on his guard duty, so he could at last lay down and close his eyes to ease the dry gritty feeling which made them so very very heavy. The dry crackle of a footstep behind him didn't alarm him. "You're early Tran." He completed his turn, expecting to see his relief. Instead, he saw the face of a man that should have been dead. His throat constricted as much from superstitious terror as from the scarred hand that grasped it, the fingers digging into the phrenic nerve as the thumb wrapped around the side of his esophagus. His death came so fast that he never heard the cracking of his neck. Casey let the body slide softly to the earth to lie under a shifting blanket of low mist. Quickly he stripped the body of its weapons and ammo. He checked the chamber of the AK-47 to make certain there was a round in the spout. The harness, with the extra magazines for the Kalashnikov Assault Rifle, was too tight to fit over the width of his shoulders. He loosened the straps so he could tie it around his waist instead. The dead Charlie's knife and canteen were also appropriated.

Casey felt a chill run over him. Turning quickly in a half crouch, the bore of the AK-47 at hip level, his eyes locked on those of the Bihnar chief squatting on the porch of his longhouse.

The two men looked at each other for a long second. Moh Chen knew that he was less than a heart beat away from death if he made the wrong move. He looked at the limp body of Doan Le Quan, gave a barely perceptible shrug of indifference, pointed to the body and then to a longhouse two buildings away. He held up his hand, showing two fingers, then slowly backed into the doorway of his hut, out of sight.

Casey gave a sigh of relief. He didn't want to kill anyone except those involved with the ambush. Besides he had always had a liking for the small tough men of the mountains and had fought side by side with them several times. He knew what Moh meant by his shrug. He would not interfere and felt no compassion for the death of the Vietnamese Bo Doi. By his signs he'd told Casey where the other Viets were sleeping and how many. He felt a bit cheated that there were only two of them here. That meant he'd missed Ho and would have to go on with the hunt.

Rifle at the ready in case he met the relief guard, he scurried across to the hut Moh Chen had pointed to, keeping to an angle where he couldn't be seen from the doorway. The longhouse, like all of them, was built about four to five feet off the earth, a single notched log serving as stairs to a small deck or porch. The walls were of woven palm fronds or thatch, as was the roof. The doorway was about half the size of a man and a single worn piece of a once red blanket hung over it, keeping out the night air. Not using the log steps, he swung his body up to lie prone on the deck. Listening for any sounds of movement from inside the hut he let his breathing ease back to normal. Through the sides, made of thin woven fronds, he could hear breathing: easy, natural, deep. The breath of those who slept with no guilt on the mind to disturb their slumber. Casey set the AK-47 down on the porch and pulled the bayonet from its sheath. The thin, slightly scratching

sound of the blade being drawn seemed unnatur-
ally loud. Staying on his belly, he slid in under the
rag of a blanket.

The interior of the hut was two shades darker
than the outside. The smell of unwashed bodies
mingled with the ever present odor of smoke from
campfires that never went out. Lying on thatch
pallets two feet apart were the sleeping forms of
the VC soldiers. They slept fully dressed, only thin
native red and black striped blankets covering
them. Scanning the room, he noted where their
weapons were lying, too close to their hands.
Packs were set against the side of the hut near a
couple of homemade crossbows. This was going to
be almost too easy. He began to move closer to the
nearest man. The weight of his body caused the
floor of the hut to creak lightly. One of the Viets
rolled over in his sleep at the sound. Casey
froze. . . .

Nothing more. He moved again, inching his
way closer to the side of the dreaming Charlie, his
bayonet in his right hand. When he reached shoulder level with his target he rose to his knees and
looked down at the smooth cheeked face. Not a
bad looking young man. Probably no more than
twenty. Mentally he sighed. Well he'll never see
twenty-one. The young Bo Doi rested on his side,
his head facing toward his comrade. Casey took a
breath, held it for a moment, let it out slowly, and
then in unison his hands struck. His left hand
slapped around the man's mouth at the same moment the bayonet hit the base of his skull severing
the nerves and sliding up under the medulla
oblongata into the brain proper. A quick painless
death that came between heart beats and was over.

There were worse ways to die. Now for the last one.

Casey was not a sadist. If he could give a man an easy death then he would. Unless he was pissed at him, that is.

Twisting the handle of the bayonet to free it from the skull, he withdrew the blade and moved around to the head of the next man. Something caused the Viet to open his eyes at the critical moment. Maybe it was the shifting of weight on the hut floor, or the sudden cessation of breathing from his comrade. Whatever it was, he wished that he had not opened his eyes in time to see the bloody blade descending. Casey left him with his throat laid open. Taking the two packs he checked them over. Inside one were a few things he could use, some fishing line and hooks and, best of all, a couple of cans of C rations taken from the dead GIs. In the other pack he found a pair of Zeiss binoculars, painted olive drab. Taking one of their weapons he returned to the opening, cautiously peering outside to make certain that no one was waiting for him. He believed the chief had told him the truth, but then who could tell for certain. There was no one there. He left the other rifle where it was. He had no use for more than one weapon. As he jumped from the porch to the earth he saw that the sun had come to life and was burning off the night mist. The air was crisp and good even though it was, as always, tinged with the smell of smoke. It was still a good smell and he felt better.

CHAPTER THREE

Moh Chen watched from the darkened entrance of his long house to see who would emerge. He felt no sense of regret when it was the long nose instead of the Vietnamese. Others from the village were beginning to emerge from the houses, women to start the cooking fires, men and children to go out to find places to ease the pressure in their bladders. By ones, then twos and threes, the word spread through the village that something out of the ordinary had taken place. The women and children returned to their longhouses, fearful that death was going to reach out and strike them. The village men of Plei Tangale waited for word from Moh to tell them what they were to do. Several had returned to their longhouses and taken out crossbows and spears. Moh said and did nothing. He waited to see what the long-nosed stranger would do first. It was odd, but he wasn't really concerned about the safety of his people. His instincts told him that they were not threatened by this scar-faced man with the bloody hands and tunic. He didn't want them and as long as he was killing Viets he couldn't be too bad.

"*Nahn do cang Ngoui Vietminh?*" Casey used the old title for the communists when he asked Moh where the other VC had gone.

Moh came down from his longhouse to squat, his finger drawing a map in the dirt. A circle represented his village and a wavy line the mountains he pointed at to the west, and a single line was the Song Cai River. On the other side of the line he placed a spatulate nail and said firmly, "Ho!"

Casey nodded his understanding. There was nothing left here for him. He'd have to go on to find Ho. The men of the Bihnar tribe lowered their primitive weapons when they saw the long nose was going to leave without making any trouble. Before leaving, Casey pointed to a left-over piece of roast dog, the hide black, charred from the fire. Moh motioned with his hand that he was welcome to it.

Casey was a bit irritated that he had lost a half day's march in his pursuit of Ho. It meant he'd have that much further to march back. Ho was heading for an area that had long been a privileged sanctuary for the communist forces. Americans were not officially allowed to cross over into either Laos or Cambodia, even if they were in hot pursuit. There had been, however, some minor excursions where the border was ill defined, or the brass had some secret purpose of their own that warranted the incursions. Casey knew that the 5th Special Forces made if not regular forays across the borders then at least frequent ones. But wherever Ho went, he'd follow. He had all the time in the world. . . .

Captain Troung was glad they were finally back in their base camp safe and sound. Here, they had the security of having an army battalion from North Vietnam to protect them as well as the added safety factor of being at the junction between South Vietnam, Cambodia and Laos. There was much to be done. Already, the first teams of Comrade Ho's *"Ke' sat Nhan,"* were being given their assignments. Some of these had been in the service of the South Vietnamese regime for years; others worked in offices, bars and barber shops. Each would be supplied with the assistance he needed to accomplish his assignment. If fighters were required they would be supplied from local resistance units and, in some cases, the Vietcong forces would take a direct part themselves if the mission called for the reduction of an entire village or armed compound. But the best form of psychological warfare would come from the fear the enemy had of never knowing if the barber he visited was going to shave him or cut his throat. Would his cook put spices or cyanide into his meal? Fear would force the enemy to make mistakes, which would further alienate the population and force them into the ranks of the Vietcong.

In the morning he would have to begin his long journey north back to Hanoi, where he would deliver by hand a copy of those selected for termination. This was too vital to be trusted to their regular messenger service, or to be transmitted by radio where there was always the chance of enemy interception. Even if the message was coded, codes could be broken.

Casey sat on the crest of a ridge overlooking Ho's camp. For the past three hours he had done nothing other than watch the camp through the Zeiss lenses. Twice he'd seen Ho going about his business, always accompanied by the same man who had been beside him at the massacre. Casey thought back to that time. In his memory he found a name—Troung! That was it. Troung must be Ho's number one boy.

The camp was strong and sentries were sharp. There was one narrow road from the north leading to the only open gate into the village and it was under the careful watch of at least two machine gun bunkers. Barbed wire and tangle foot, probably mixed with booby traps and mines, were strung in three aprons around the perimeter, with low watchtowers on all corners. It reminded him a lot of some of the Special Forces camps he'd visited. It would be hard for him to get himself into the camp without being spotted. He'd have to get Ho to come out after him.

Casey spent the next two days avoiding Viet patrols and finding something to eat. He wanted to save his two precious cans of rations for later if he had to run for it and didn't have time to forage. His main staple was raw fish from the river. This was not a place to build a camp fire. Cold meat was all he'd have till he got out of here.

Never spending the night in the same place, he moved his observation posts from one site to another every day. Several times he'd crept down close to the camp to get a closer look at its defenses, but was not encouraged by what he saw and heard. Even though the Viets were in what they believed to be a safe area, the guards weren't lax and security was tight. It was on the third day of his watch that he saw several groups of men and a few women come and go, all of them with escorts. Something was up. Through his glasses he could see that most of comrade Ho's guests didn't have the look of soldiers about them. They were up to something. But what?

On the fourth day he sat on a rocky ledge and saw a French made Citroen come into the camp. Troung came out and put a suitcase in it then moved to the hut where Ho kept his office. Casey thought about it for a moment. This could be his break. If Troung was going to leave the camp, then perhaps . . .

Ho walked with his trusted aide to the car. "Comrade, give my best regards to General Giap and the members of his staff. Tell them all is going according to plan and we should have positive results very soon." Into Troung's hands he placed a folder containing the names of those who had been selected for death. Troung put these in his briefcase and locked it, then handcuffed the case to his own wrist. It would not leave him till he reached Hanoi.

The road from the camp was secure. There had never been any trouble on it and if there was there were regular strong points along the way where Troung could receive aid if needed. With Troung, Ho sent three of his best men as bodyguards. They would readily give their lives for him before they failed in the mission to protect Troung and the papers he carried.

Troung settled into the unfamiliar luxury of the plush car seats of the Citroen. To have such a vehicle for his journey was significant of the importance of his mission. He was singularly honored to have such a responsibility entrusted to him. It was most certainly a high mark of favor. In the front seat with him were the driver on one side and one guard on the other who watched the road ahead of them on either side. Though it was a bit cramped with their weapons, behind him were the other two men who were responsible for his safety. The camp disappeared from sight in less than a minute as they rounded a curve that led into the cool shadows of overhanging trees laced with lush vines and flowers.

Troung closed his eyes to get some badly needed sleep. There had not been much rest since they had returned. He was just in that half-asleep zone, where reality and dreams sometimes overlap, when the front of the Citroen lept into the air followed by a dull crumping noise. It took less than half a second for Troung to rally his senses and know what had taken place. A grenade had exploded. The driver of the car frantically tried to regain control of his careening vehicle as it spun out on the road and crashed into a wall of trees, driving his head through the windshield. The guard riding shotgun tried to get the door open only to have his face ripped off by a burst of automatic fire. Troung's two guards in the rear seat both hit their doors at the same time firing and rolling to try and get whoever it was that was shooting at them to reveal his position. Troung covered up, ducking down behind the seat. There were a couple of quick bursts of fire, glass blew out from the rear window, and thousands of minute shards covered the back like diamond dust. Then it was quiet. A voice made him raise his head.

"Comrade Troung, I believe?" Troung wiped blood from his forehead amazed that he wasn't hurt and terrified of who might be speaking to him. The accent wasn't Vietnamese. A hand jerked him from the back seat and onto the road, where he stumbled over the body of one of his guards to land on his knees. He knew the others in his party were dead too. For the first time he got a good look at the face behind the voice. His bladder released itself and warm urine ran down the inside of his pants leg.

"Don't cry little man. As you can see I'm not dead and neither are you—yet." Casey pointed the muzzle of the AK-47 at the briefcase. "What do you have in there that's so important?" Troung said nothing, just clasped the briefcase close to his thin chest.

"Give it to me," Casey demanded. Troung shook his head croaking out, "I don't have the key."

Casey grinned evilly. "Then that is too bad for you." He kicked Troung under the chin. It was always easier to work with an unconscious patient. From his belt he took his bayonet and tested the edge with a thumb. It would do.

Troung was found by a patrol that had heard the shots and rushed to the scene. They found only dead men and Troung lying in the dust of the road. A tourniquet around Troung's left wrist had kept him from bleeding to death. His hand and the precious briefcase with its list of targets was gone.

By radio the nearest VC center was contacted and a truck was sent out to the site of the ambush. Troung was in a half coma, snapping out of it now and then to scream in agony at the burning in his hand. He tried to move his missing fingers but they wouldn't bend or respond to his commands. Then he'd pass out again.

Ho had been informed by radio of what had happened. As soon as he'd got the word of Troung's ambush and the missing briefcase he'd ordered massive patrolling to find the assailant and if possible bring him back alive. But at all costs they were to recover the briefcase.

Back at camp, Troung was unloaded with care, his body placed on a stretcher and taken to the hut which served as a dispensary for the Vietcong troops. Ho was there waiting for him with the regimental doctor he had sent for from the 126th PAVN.

Ho bent over the stretcher. Troung was unconscious. Drawing his hand back he gave his aide a slap which could have been heard fifty meters away. The shock of the slap brought Troung's eyes half open.

"How many ambushed you and who were they? Vietnamese or Americans? Which way did they go?"

Troung tried to speak but his voice was weak. Bending over to place his ear by Troung's lips, Ho's eyes grew wide with disbelief. "Impossible. It could not be the same man. He was dead. Absolutely dead. It must have been someone who looked like him." Troung shook his head weakly from side to side then passed out again. Ho left Troung to the care of the doctor and went back outside to the compound and looked to the mountains surrounding his post. A cold chill ran up his spine as he felt that other eyes, pale, gray-blue eyes, were also watching him.

CHAPTER FOUR

Casey lowered the binoculars from his eyes. He would have preferred to wait a bit longer to get a clearer shot at Ho, but things had changed since he'd gotten his hands on the papers in Troung's briefcase and this was the best he could hope for right now. Gauging the distance to be about four hundred meters, he sighted downhill about two feet above Ho's head, took in the slack on the trigger and fired off a three round burst. Ho hit the dirt. One of the Russian made 7.62 rounds clipped his right shoulder. The other two only served to add impetus to his hands and feet as he scurried for cover.

"Shit!" grumbled Casey. "If I'd had a decent Springfield or Mauser I'd have taken the son of a bitch's head off."

From the Viet camp, return fire began to come up the hill. They didn't know exactly where he was but they could still get lucky. A mortar round exploded forty feet in front of him, sending shards of white hot shrapnel whistling through the branches of the trees. Time to get hat and get gone. He'd had his chance and blew it. Now he had to take the papers he'd gotten from Troung and get them back to Intelligence. His Vietnamese wasn't the best, but he could tell from the list of names in the documents that they were very important. He'd have to try for Ho again later.

Colonel Ho van Tuyen was very upset. Not only had his best man been mutilated but he himself had very nearly been killed.

"Get him!" he screamed in a combination of fright and anger.

"Tieu' die't Nguoi ban trom!" His order to kill the sniper wasn't going to be an easy one to obey. Casey had already vacated the vicinity and was heading back east. He'd have to move carefully at least till nightfall. He'd seen the patrols being sent out and knew they'd been drawn by the sounds of his gunfire.

Ho had his wound treated. It was painful if not serious. The bullet had burned a groove through the thin meat covering the tip of his right shoulder socket. After he had been treated he left Troung to the sometimes less than tender ministrations of the doctor and took to the hunt himself, taking his own personal bodyguards with him. He still didn't believe Troung's story that the man who had taken the Kill List was the same one they'd left for dead. He believed Troung must be suffering from shock and having hallucinations.

Casey moved smoothly, easily through the brush and trees, letting his instincts guide his steps to take the line of least resistance. He didn't try to fight his way through. Instead he moved with the terrain, not rushing it. He measured himself and his strength. He had one advantage. He knew for certain which way he was going and the Viets didn't. Until he was spotted he'd have the edge.

At the Song Cai he changed direction and headed north, rather than taking the crossing. He figured the Viets would most likely think he'd try to get across the river as fast as possible to get back to the South Vietnamese side of the border. Traveling about an hour, he found a spot to hole up in—a thick cluster of bamboo, the shoots measuring the thickness of his arm. Twisting his way inside he settled down to wait. Let the Viets run after him in the dark and wear themselves out. He'd make the river crossing after dawn and cut around them.

Twice, before darkness fell, he heard the hunters searching for him as they spread out along the riverbank looking for any sign of their elusive prey. From behind the cluster of bamboo he watched them enter the brown waters of the Sia-kuang and wade over to the other side.

Good, let them all get in front of him and he'd be at their rear. As they advanced to the east, they'd have to spread themselves thinner and thinner, making gaps between them that he should be able to slip through without too much trouble. With a sigh, he opened one of his cans of rations and dined on the meal he hated most: cold ham and lima beans.

Concealing his body from view by burrowing deep into a nest of leaves, he slept. Near midnight, when the Southern Cross was high in the Asian sky, he woke. Lying there, he looked to the skies above him, the stars cold and distant. He listened. A thousand different sounds came to him. He heard the croaking of tree frogs and the rustle of leaves in the high trees as night creatures of a hundred shapes hunted, fed and bred in their endless cycle of life, death and procreation. Uncovering himself he rolled over, then rose slowly to his feet, his body stiff, joints cracking. He waited again to let his senses take in all that was around him so that he would know which things were natural and which caused by man. The briefcase in his left hand, the AK in his right, its safety off, a round in the chamber, he left the bamboo thicket and moved to the river. Lightning rumbled in the distance. Like an artillery barrage it rolled over the crest of the mountains, momentarily lighting up the horizon, then disappeared as the dark returned till the next assault. Wading into the black waters felt good. He waded deeper, keeping his weapon at the ready. At no point did the river climb above his waist, but he knew that if the rains moved this way the river could change in seconds into a raging torrent.

On the South Vietnamese side of the river he paused, listened, used his peripheral vision to check for anything that moved in the maze of shadows that was the tree line in front of him. Nothing! With only the dull roar of his own heart beating the pulse in his temple, he moved forward in the covering shelter of the jungle. The enemy couldn't see any better at night than he could and there were more of them to make mistakes and sounds as they coughed or bumped their weapons. The going was slow. But this was no time to rush.

Ho sat beside the only fire he permitted that night. He had made camp several kilometers behind his lead patrols. The wound in his shoulder had become quite painful and had made him a bit feverish. Legs crossed in front of him, he went over a map of the area. The map, like most of those available, was less than complete, even though he had painstakingly hand drawn in many of the terrain features himself. It was hard to concentrate and he was furious. His men had found no sign of the sniper. From radio reports he didn't think that a helicopter could have come in and extricated him. He had to be somewhere in the vicinity. In the morning he would send out to the Montagnard villagers for trackers. He still had patrols out on every trail he knew of, though there were always some approaches that only the natives knew, but he would find those too. The heat thunder from the heights was no comfort to him. It mocked him as if it were the voices of the "Than Tien," the spirits of the mountains. His shoulder throbbed and he was tired, but he couldn't sleep. He had to get that list back. It was a matter of honor, not that he really cared that much if the enemy found out that some of them were marked for death. That might even help in his battle for their minds. True, it could make some of the kills a bit more difficult, but for those he could always select alternate targets. He was not a man who was completely rigid in his thinking. To be adaptable to changing circumstances was always a most admirable trait, and he did certainly consider himself to be an admirable man in all respects. But he would have the swine who shot him, even if it meant going into MACV headquarters for him. He would find out who it was that had dared to come so far into a country that he, Ho, considered his personal domain.

Casey stopped for a breather to gather his bearings. During this interval he took enough time to slip the briefcase handle through his belt so it would hang at his back bumping into his butt and leaving both his hands free.

From a ridge Casey saw the glow of a camp fire over the trees, a reddish light that waved and moved.

"Shit!" he grumbled to himself. He would have to pass close to the camp if he was going to get clear. This was the most critical junction, where winding tortured valleys and gorges turned back on themselves into a maze. If he varied from his course, it might take days to correct. He would have to go straight on. Still, it might not present too much of a problem. The Charlies were probably looking for him far to the front. If he was careful he'd most likely be able to get by them without being spotted.

Moving carefully, as silent as possible, he placed one foot in front of the other on the thin animal trail that served as a road through the jungle. Holding the AK-47 in front of him, he tried to gauge the distance he'd advanced against that to the camp fire. He'd lost sight of the red glow since he'd entered the forest. The smell of wood smoke drifted to him. He could still be a hundred meters away or two hundred; he couldn't tell. But whatever the distance was it was now time to get off the trail. This close to them it would be wishful thinking to imagine they didn't have any sentries set out. He didn't like having to move through the thick brush off the trail, but he had no choice. It would take a lot longer but it was safer.

The next hundred meters took him nearly an hour to travel. Every step he was forced to push or duck under vines and branches, several times getting on his hands and knees to crawl beneath the thick interwoven branches of thickets. Sweat poured from every pore, his mouth sticky and foul tasting. If he'd been able to see, salt sweat would have blinded him. But as it was, he could see nothing. Only his instincts led him in the right direction. The smell of smoke became stronger. He could hear voices speaking normally. He was quite close to the camp. Closer than he'd wanted to be. He decided to take a chance and crawled closer to the sound of the voices.

From where he lay under the cover of a thick clump of brush at the edge of a small clearing, he could see the Viet camp. There were three men sitting by the fire, and barely visible on the far side of the camp he could make out at least two more men walking the perimeter of the clearing. There would be others nearby. He started to pull back, scuttling his legs and arms in reverse. Then he froze. He had pulled back just far enough under the bush to where he couldn't see anything. Footsteps crackling on leaves and twigs had stopped his retreat.

Ho grunted in pain as his shoulder moved when he undid the zipper of his khaki trousers. The night was warm but not overly so. It would get worse before the monsoons came. He was still thinking of the monsoons when he emptied his bladder on the bush at the edge of his camp.

The sudden unexpected shower of hot urine on his back caused a spontaneous grunt from Casey. He was caught! Jumping to his feet to stand in the middle of the bush he tried to get his AK-47 raised up to at least hip level where he could spray the camp and the son of bitch who'd just taken a leak on his back.

Both stared at each other in surprise. The light of the camp fire clearly showed Casey's face. The scar, running from his eye to the corner of his mouth, looked even deeper than Ho remembered it being. Ho let loose of his now shriveled organ as it reacted on its own accord and tried to retreat back up into his groin. Casey cursed at the brush which kept him from being able to raise the assault rifle up high enough for him to at least kill the man in front of him. It was almost as big a shock to him when he made out the features of Ho. He hadn't been able to see at first, because the light of the camp fire was behind the Viet.

Ho screamed like a wounded pig and hit the ground, his fly still open and his shriveled organ getting badly scratched as he crawled on his belly away from the bush. His cries brought the sentries. Casey swore at them, dropped back down in the brush to his knees and at last let loose with a long hosing burst of full automatic fire that knocked the kneecaps off one of the Viets and slowed the others down. He broke free of the bush and began to run as fast as he could, ignoring the whipping lashes of thorn vines and brush that tore at his clothes and flesh.

Bursts of machine gun fire rattled after him ripping gouges out of tree trunks. He hit the trail by accident. This time he made no effort to get off of it. Running as fast as his legs would take him, lungs heaving, he rounded a bend to find he was running through the center of a VC outpost. His AK took out two guards. Both had been kneeling behind an RPD light machine gun set up behind a log facing east. As he cleared the log, several shots came from his rear as the pursuing Viets tried to close the gap. Running till he could hear no more sounds of anyone on his trail he slowed to where his heart, after threatening to leave his chest, finally eased back to a mere chest crushing throb.

Ho was in a near state of shock. Troung had not been having hysterical delusions. The man who had cut off his hand was the one they had killed. No! He had it wrong. He wasn't a superstitious peasant. He was an educated man who knew better. If the scar-faced sergeant was still alive, then it was only because he hadn't died and they had not really killed him. There had been many men who had survived wounds that looked to be fatal. Still he had looked awfully dead. Trying to reconcile what he knew against what he had seen was too much. Ho gave it up. To continue that line of thought would only lead to madness. It was enough that the scar-faced one might still be alive, but if so, he would see to it that the mistake would soon be corrected.

By dawn, Casey had outdistanced the VC. He was well ahead of them entering onto one of the plateaus scattered about the highlands, leaving the jungle behind and below him in the valleys. Here, the terrain resembled some parts of the American southwest, with broad and flat grasslands. By noon, with the sun high in the sky, heat waves had begun to shimmer and quiver in the distance. Twice he had heard the sounds of aircraft overhead: a flight of fighter bombers heading southeast, probably going back to Ton son Nhut airbase outside Saigon, and once the droning of an old C-46 heading toward Laos. It probably belonged to Air America and was making a hard rice drop, as munitions were called, to the Meo tribesmen in the mountains around the Plaines Des Jars.

Two hours later a flight of three Hueys and two

gunboats passed over escorting a dust-off chopper
carrying two wounded Special Forces men from
the camp at Cheo Reo to the hospital at Dalat.
Casey waved his arms frantically at the helicopters. He thought they'd missed him when one of
the gunboats made a sharp sliding turn to pass
right overhead. The doorgunner kept the sights of
the M-60 on the man below till it was clear that he
wasn't a Viet. The dust-off gained some altitude
and orbited as the other gunboat provided security
till its brother ship had touched down and taken
aboard their unexpected passenger. Casey didn't
care where they were going as long as there was a
bath and bed there.

Ho stood concealed at the edge of the plateau
watching the flight of helicopters take Casey away
from him. This did not end the chase. Ho had
promised himself that he'd have that scar-faced
swine even if it meant going into MACV itself,
and he would. He signaled to his men to turn
back. He had many things to do this day.

CHAPTER FIVE

The chopper hadn't completely settled down on the perforated steel-plated landing zone inside the relative safety of the compound before Casey was ducking under the blades, which to him always looked as if they were going to take his head off. He still carried the AK-47 he'd taken off the Charlie he'd snuffed at the Bihnar village. Intelligence would probably want to check the serial numbers and see where it came from, Russia or China. Captain Delfino Gomez, a slightly built, curly-haired man whose bloodlines showed the strains of Castile and who was a onetime native of Leadville, Colorado, motioned over the sound of the rotors for Casey to come to him. As Casey neared him the Captain's eyes said, *Goddamn, that son of a bitch looks like he's been through the mill.* "Are you okay Sergeant? Do you want to go to the dispensary before reporting to the old man?" Gomez's stare went to the holes in Casey's tunic and the blood stains. Before he could ask the obvious, Casey beat him to the punch. "That's not my blood, Captain. I'm all right. If you want I'll check in with the medics later." Casey knew from long practice that it worked best if you just gave them something they could understand and relate to. Even if they didn't quite believe you it

usually took too much mental effort for them to
pursue a line of questioning that was awkward or
silly sounding.

Gomez led him over to a jeep, climbed in the
driver's seat and started the motor. He had seen
Casey around from time to time but had never had
much to do with the man, other than give an occasional order which was always acknowledged by
the sergeant with as few words as possible. It was a
bit difficult to resist the temptation to question
him during their ride over to Battalion HQ, but he
knew that Colonel Tomlin would get pissed off if
he did. The short ride from the chopper pad across
the compound gave Casey a chance to try and get
his story straight. The colonel was no fool and
he'd want specific answers. A column of ten Armored Personnel Carriers passed them, heading
for the gate to join in a search and destroy operation around the base of the mountains to the east
of Kontum.

Captain Gomez pulled the olive drab jeep into
the spot reserved for him at HQ. Casey followed
him into the white painted building that had once
served the French as a school house. Casey ignored the slightly distasteful and questioning
looks from the office personnel. They took great
pride in having a neat and clean office operation
and didn't like to have it tracked up by derelicts.

Captain Gomez told the colonel's secretary,
Sp/4 Amos Ferguson, a former rifleman who
could type over a hundred words a minute and was
therefore too valuable for line duty, even though
he requested it once a week, to announce their
presence.

Colonel Tomlin had the look and manner of a

southern lawyer, which he had been prior to Korea. His eyes were narrow, mouth calculating, with thin lips, but not without some humor. He was now a professional military man who had given up a not so thriving law practice to stay in the military and had found that his talents were much better suited to the gathering and interpretation of intelligence than they were to trying to get some dope dealer off the hook.

He had read Casey's file and had a number of questions that he wanted answered. Besides, he wanted to know where the son of a bitch had been for the last two weeks, especially now that he had acquired the documents which were lying in front of him. He hadn't had a chance to get a full translation, but from what had been translated he knew that the fecal matter was about to come in contact with the rotating oscillator. . . .

"Enter." He liked short sharp single word commands. Casey and Captain Gomez presented themselves in front of his desk and reported. Tomlin never took his eyes off the documents in front of him. He dismissed Gomez with an off-hand acknowledgement of his salute and turned his attention to Casey as the door to his office closed behind the captain.

"At ease sergeant, and take a seat. I'll be with you in a moment." Casey did as he was instructed and settled heavily into a plush leather chair. Tomlin was trying to get his questions in order, besides which he had learned that silence on the part of a superior was often a ploy when it came to gaining the psychological advantage over underlings. From beneath the captured documents he removed another file. Casey's 201. In it was all

that was known of the man sitting in his office
smelling up the room with the odor of an unwashed body, wood smoke and God knows what
else.

The personnel file in front of him did nothing to
set his mind at ease. There were too many holes in
it, too many things unanswered that made his
lawyer's mind pick up speed. Yes indeed! A most
interesting file.

He raised his eyes to those of the sergeant and
still said nothing. This was a practiced and effective move that put the object of his attention in a
state of unease and inflicted guilt feelings, whether
the man had done anything or not, and Tomlin,
having practiced law in Nashville, Tennessee knew
that everyone had always done something. It was
just a matter of finding out what it was. This
technique quite often brought answers to questions he hadn't even asked or thought of.

Casey returned his gaze with disinterest. He
knew what the colonel was trying to do and locked
his own eyes on those of the superior officer.
Tomlin suddenly felt uneasy under the return gaze
of the somehow unsettling gray-blue eyes that
looked back at him with such disinterest. It was a
feeling that he wasn't used to. Clearing his throat,
he shifted the weight on his ass from one cheek to
the other and broke the eye contact with the distinct feeling that he had been bested. He didn't
like it much.

"Sergeant, just where and how did you come to
gain possession of these documents?" He indicated the captured papers with a miniature
chrome-plated bayonet letter opener. Casey kept
his story simple, saying only that he'd managed to

escape the ambush then had followed after the VC
till he was able to catch, and in the process, take
the papers off an enemy officer. Tomlin tried to
query him on details but gained little for his efforts, other than what had already been said. On a
chart, Casey indicated the area he thought he'd
been in and the route he'd taken in and out of the
Song Cai River valley.

Tomlin resisted the impulse to explore the situation further. There was a time and place for everything and sometimes the stage had to be set first.

"From your file, Sergeant, I see that you are
not American born and enlisted under a French
passport. The only thing that Intelligence has
come up with on you is that you served with the
French Foreign Legion here in the fifties and had
fought at Dien Bien Phu. Is that correct?"

Casey nodded his agreement. Tomlin pursed his
lips, cleared his throat and went on. "Now as to
your place of birth and the date you gave us, some
facts were not possible to check out, such as the
city in Germany that you say is your birth place. It
no longer exists and there is no way to check you
out any further. What do you have to say about
that?"

Casey leaned slightly forward. "When I was
discharged from the Étrangère I was given, as
you know, a new passport and French citizenship.
As to where I was born, or when, that is my concern and will remain in the past where it belongs.
When I enlisted I made it clear that I was not
going to give any information about my past other
than my service with the French army. At that
time, the Americans were in need of people who
had experience in this region of the world and we

came to an agreement that my passport was all that was needed for the purposes of identification. I see no reason to change that agreement now."

Tomlin knew that there were several hundred, if not several thousand, others serving in the American Armed Forces who had fought with other armies, some of them hostile to the interests of the United States at one time or another. Many of them were what was known as DPs, Displaced Persons left over from World War Two, or like this man, one who had served in the French Foreign Legion in order to gain a new identity and passport which made them legal citizens of their host country.

Casey pointed a dirty fingernail at the documents on the colonel's desk. "Have you gone through all of them yet?"

"No! Just enough to know that these are very important."

"Then, Colonel, I suggest you take a look at the third page under the heading of *Nguoi My*, about halfway down the page."

Tomlin did as Casey instructed. His heart skipped a beat when he saw his own name in a list of about thirty others under the Vietnamese heading of "Americans."

Casey spoke again, his voice low and earnest. "I really don't think you need to know any more about me other than that I am on your side. And I am the only one here who knows what Ho looks like. Let me have my head and I'll bring you his, and probably save yours." Tomlin felt a sudden chill race up his spine to settle in the nape of his neck. It was not pleasant to see your name among others who had been scheduled to die. The normal risks of war were bad enough without being singled out for extermination. His interest in the scar-faced sergeant's past was now something he could care less about.

"What do you mean Sergeant Romain? I mean about giving you your head?" The words were slightly choked.

Casey rose from his chair and turned his back to the colonel. "I want you to put me on detached duty and let me go where I want when I want. I'll either capture or kill Ho for you and . . ." he paused, "for myself. I have a personal thing to settle with him."

Tomlin had spent enough years listening to the tones in men's voices to know that Casey was in deadly earnest and right now that was to his advantage. "I'll think about it, Sergeant. For now, go get yourself cleaned up and rested. I'll talk to you again tomorrow. Be here at 0900 hours."

As Casey left the office, again in the company of Captain Gomez, he heard the colonel bellowing for his interpreter to get his ass in the office and finish translating "these goddamned papers" before he had the little bastard reassigned to the ARVIN as a rifleman. Tomlin shoved Casey's file back into a drawer. He was no longer interested in what the man had done in the past as much as what he could do in the future.

Gomez climbed back into the seat of the jeep and hit the starter, pausing a moment before shifting into gear. "What now, sergeant? Where do we go from here?"

Casey bummed a smoke from him, lit up and inhaled deeply. "Wherever I can clean up and get something to eat. I'm supposed to see Colonel

Tomlin again in the morning, so anywhere you put me will be all right.''

Gomez nodded, put the jeep in reverse, pulled out and headed for the transient barracks, which would do for now.

By the time Casey had had the incredible luxury of a hot shower, Gomez had arranged for a clean uniform to be issued and delivered from supply to the transient barracks, where those waiting for reassignment or shipment back to the states were being processed. There were a few like Casey who were just stopping there for a day or two on their way to someplace else. Gomez left Casey to his own devices after loaning him ten dollars so he could get a few personal things like a razor and cigarettes. After a lunch in the mess hall of sausage and potatoes, which tasted as if they had been prepared in the states and shipped over two weeks ago, Casey went back to the transient barracks, lowered the blinds on the small window, stripped down and lay his body between clean sheets. He'd sleep through till the next morning, then he'd settle with the colonel. He knew the type well enough and had little doubt that Tomlin would see the wisdom of his suggestion now that he knew his own ass was on the line.

Tomlin's interpreter, Minh tran Quan, had been in the service of the American forces for three years and had been a good and valuable aid to them. A small man, with the manners of a brow-beaten accountant, he always deferred to all the Americans he met, always smiling and bobbing his head up and down, making his Adam's apple do tricks. Minh had been expecting his current master's demand that he make an appearance and had prepared for it. As always he had his old brown leather briefcase with him. Grinning his way past the colonel's infantryman secretary, he entered Tomlin's office to be greeted by a barrage of questions and accusations.

"You little slope headed son of a bitch! Why didn't you tell me that my name was on the damned list? Have you lost your mind entirely? What the hell do we pay you for anyway, you incompetent little twit?"

Minh bowed his head in acceptance of the rebuke being heaped upon him. Smiling his most ingratiating grin he answered Tomlin's questions with no trace of having heard the insulting tones.

"I wished it to be a surprise for you, sir."

"Surprise! You wanted it to be a surprise?" Tomlin half rose from behind his desk. "Now just what makes you think you have the right to determine what will be a surprise and what will not?" Minh nodded his head up and down as before, opened his briefcase and froze the colonel in his half-raised position.

The clicking of the hammer being drawn back to full cock on the American made Colt 45 automatic pistol sounded as loud as a 60 mm mortar round explosion.

"It is quite simple, sir. You see, you belong to me."

Tomlin closed his eyes, knowing what was going to happen next.

Spannng! The powerful explosion of a pistol going off deafened him. But where was the pain? The shock of a heavy caliber slug tearing through his flesh? He opened one eye tentatively. Minh lay face up five feet away from where he'd opened his briefcase. The front of his face was gone. Brains and bone splinters littered the top of Tomlin's desk.

Amos stood in the doorway, a crowd of office workers gathering behind him, his own forty-five giving off a wisp of blue tinged smoke from the breech. "You know, sir. I never did trust that little shit very much. Now can I have my transfer to a line company?"

Tomlin's legs had turned to water. He collapsed heavily back into his overstuffed chair. Weakly, he croaked out an answer to Amos' question. "Yes! Certainly! Anything you want."

"Thank you, sir." Amos put the safety back on the pistol and returned to his desk to write up his new request for reassignment.

CHAPTER SIX

For Tomlin, after the initial shock had worn off and he had come to grips with the realization that he was not among the immortals, it had been a soul shattering experience. He had gained a new fondness and appreciation for his life. All other considerations of the war took a distant second place to his own survival. What was it Sergeant Romain had said?

"I am the only one here who knows what Ho looks like. Let me have my head and I'll bring you his, and probably save yours."

The colonel spent the next hours, and half the next morning making the necessary arrangements to see that Sgt. Romain could indeed have his head. Tomlin had to pull a lot of strings and call in several IOUs at MACV, but at this point in life there was no price too great to pay.

The news of Tomlin's near assassination spread over the compound and was greeted with responses ranging from "He was a lucky bastard" to expressed sympathy that the interpreter had missed his chance to rid the world of an asshole. It was, therefore, with little surprise to Casey that he was once again summoned to Tomlin's office. This time his appearance was more to the liking of the office staff. A shave and a clean uniform took years off his appearance. Captain Gomez was already there when he arrived.

"Good morning, Sergeant. The colonel's waiting for us." Casey acknowledged the greeting with a nod of his head and followed Gomez into Tomlin's sanctum sanctorum.

Both were granted permission to sit. Tomlin stroked his chin with his fingers, knowing this gave him a thoughtful and learned countenance that added import to his words.

"Gentlemen! I have made some arrangements pursuant to our conversation of yesterday. Sgt. Romain, I have decided that you were correct in your assessments. It seems that you are right in that you are the only one we know of who has seen Colonel Ho. I have checked with all of our intelligence agencies to see if anyone else has a file or photograph of him, and there is nothing other than some general information as to his family background and education. I shall, in due course, make that file available to you both. I say both, because as of this date, you are both relieved from any other duties and are to devote yourselves to finding and terminating our good Comrade Ho, and any of his operatives you may come in contact with."

Tomlin cleared his throat and stood, his back to the office window. His scalp tingled as the thought of being silhouetted in the window frame passed through his mind. He took one large step sideways, taking him away from the exposed window and, he hoped, unobtrusively nearer the wall map of Vietnam, as if that had been his sole purpose in moving.

"As of this date, you are both on TDY (temporary duty) to an organization known as the Phoenix Project, a clandestine group, oriented toward the disruption of the enemy's infrastructure, through whatever means the situation warrants."

Both Casey and Gomez knew the colonel meant they were to kill the enemy without having the normal restrictions of war placed on them. They would be able to "Terminate with Extreme Prejudice" anyone they suspected of being involved with Ho's *Ke' sat Nhan* teams.

Tomlin set a gimlet eye on his two subordinates. "Now this is the way it works. Romain, you requested that you be given your head. You have it. However, from this moment on your control officer will be Captain Gomez. Coordinate your actions and requests through him. Do you at this time have any special requests?"

Casey and Gomez looked at each other. Casey was content with the situation. Gomez seemed to be a cool, steady, realistic type who didn't have any great deal of respect for the military's normal line of bullshit. He'd be all right to work with, but he needed something more.

"Yes, sir. I would like it if you could have a *Luc Long Dac Biet* officer named Van tran Tuyen assigned to me. I've worked with him before and I'll need him to interpret for me, as well as provide a backup I can depend on if needed." Tomlin recalled his own recent experience with a South Vietnamese he trusted, and even though the LLDB was the South Vietnamese equivalent of the US Special Forces he had developed a sudden distrust of all Orientals. "Do you think he's reliable, Sergeant?"

Casey nodded his head. "No problem there, Colonel. I'd bet my life on it."

Tomlin grimaced mentally, *Not just your life but mine, which is infinitely more important.* "Very well Sergeant, I'll see what I can do. Give his name to my orderly and I'll check him out for you. Anything else?"

Casey nodded, "I'll need to be able to pick my own weapons, and I'll need some gold, probably a couple of thousand dollars worth to start with."

Tomlin and Gomez both looked at him as if he were mad. "Just what the hell do you need with gold, Sergeant? You're not going to open up an account in Switzerland are you?"

For the first time Casey laughed easily in the colonel's presence. "No, but I will need help that I don't think you would be able to supply. There is a Cambodian Kamserai chieftain named Phang that I would like to put on the payroll. He has the means to supply me with up to date information on Vietcong activities and their whereabouts. Also, he's not restricted by the border and has enough men to put up a hell of a fight when necessary, and it will probably be necessary, especially across the border, if we have to go back into Laos or Cambodia after Ho. I'm sure you'll agree that a border fight between Kamserai bandits and the Vietcong would cause less of an international outcry than an incursion in force by American or South Vietnamese units?"

Tomlin grudgingly agreed to Casey's demands. "I'll see to it, but you had better show me some results, and quickly, if you expect to continue in this matter." To Gomez he directed his next words, which dripped with heavy emphasis.

"You, Captain, are in charge. Get the details as to how to contact this Kamserai bandit. What's his name? Phang? Just remember anything that goes wrong will be your direct responsibility. Any further communication from Sgt. Romain will come through you. Is that clear?"

Gomez agreed that it was. He knew the reason why he was put in charge. If things went wrong it would be his ass that was hung out to dry and, if it went well, then Tomlin would reap the benefits. Everything was normal. They were dismissed with an offhand wave.

Both were relieved to be out in the open again. Being around the former attorney too long gave both a slightly oily feeling, as if they had just been conned in some manner. Perhaps Tomlin's short career around the criminal element had contaminated him to some degree to where he couldn't trust a straight deal. Gomez and Casey had both known types like that.

They walked together across the compound. "What do you think will be your first move, Sergeant?"

"I won't know that till I get Van here, and locate old Phang, the Kamserai. Once that's done, I'll be ready to move. It's too early to make any kind of definitive plan. As I see it, we have only two choices. One, we go after Ho, or two, we make Ho come to us. And I wouldn't be surprised if he has already made plans to do just that."

Colonel Ho van Tuyen spoke with emphasis as he directed his one-handed aide: "From this moment on your duties will consist solely of locating the one who crippled you and humiliated me. Use

our agents to find him. That shouldn't be too difficult. I have already received a communication
from Kontum that one of our agents was killed at-
tempting to assassinate an American Intelligence
officer. A sergeant answering our man's descrip-
tion was with the Intelligence officer the same day.
As I see it, we have two choices in this matter. We
can go and get him or make him come to us.
Either one will suit me well enough, as long as he
is in my hands before the month is out.''

Troung agreed. Now that he had a mission he
would, as always, see it through. He, like Ho, had
managed to convince himself that he had been
mistaken about the scar-faced American's death.
Now that the matter was cleared up he could go
about his business with a clear mind. When next
he had the American in his power, he would put to
rest any lingering doubts that might remain buried
in the depths of his subconscious mind.

Troung arranged to have a meeting set up with
one of his more effective agents in the Kontum
area. He would go himself to see that the job was
properly done. This operation had taken on a personal aspect. He owed the American for both the
loss of his hand and much of his self-respect. He
was grateful that Comrade Ho had shown such
understanding in the matter. It would not have
been unusual for Ho to have ordered him executed for a failure of such magnitude. He would
not fail his master again.

Captain Gomez and Casey sat in the transient
barracks talking over their options. Casey told
Gomez how to get in touch with Phang through a
Chinese merchant that the old bastard dealt with

on a regular basis. All he had to do was give the
Chinese Casey's name and where he could be contacted and Phang would do the rest. As for Van,
all that was necessary was for someone to call
LLDB Headquarters in Saigon on Rue Le Van
Diet and they'd be able to get in touch with him.
Casey warned Gomez not to divulge the reason
they wished Van assigned to them. Even the Vietnamese Special Forces were known to have their
full share of enemy agents in their midst, though
they were a bit more secure than the ARVIN
forces. Gomez agreed. He arranged through the
commander of the 5th Special Forces Group Vietnam to have Van come to them by way of personal
request from one commander to another. This
wouldn't be very difficult, as they and the SF men
now had much in common. The Phoenix Operation had many of the Green Bereted jungle experts
in their ranks.

Gomez avoided the temptation to question his
new associate about his past, instinctively knowing the man would give him nothing. He had read
Casey's 201 himself and, while the man's past had
many gaps in it, what they had been able to find
out from friends in the Deuxième Bureau about
his service with the French forces gave them no
reason to doubt his hatred for the communists. It
had been proven by his many decorations while
in the service of the French in Indochina and
Algeria. In a strange manner he didn't feel
superior in rank to the sergeant and knew that
he'd do well to listen, more than talk. He didn't
know where Romain had come from and, at this
point, didn't really care. He didn't think he was
German, though his file said he was born there

and he spoke it fluently. He also spoke French, English and even Vietnamese to some degree. The more holes he found in Romain's history, the more fascinating the subject became. As to their future association, he would wait and see. If Romain decided to tell him more, then he would listen. He knew there was nothing he could do to threaten a man like this. Threats of a court-martial or bad assignments would mean less than nothing to him. Romain had something in back of his eyes that went beyond the more mundane penalties of a contemporary military existence. Whatever was going to come down now, Gomez would readily have given odds, it was going to be entertaining and deadly.

CHAPTER SEVEN

It took the better part of a week before Gomez could relay to Casey that Tomlin had sent for the Kamserai chieftain, Phang. He would be brought to them in a couple of days. Right now the arrangements were being made for a chopper pickup. As for his Vietnamese friend, even though he applied all the pressure he could, Van was not available. He was on an operation and couldn't be released at this time. However LLDB Headquarters in Saigon had promised him that as soon as he finished his mission they would assign him to Colonel Tomlin and the Phoenix Project.

Colonel Ho van Tuyen was not waiting for anyone. He gave the orders for the *Ke' sat Nhan* to go into an operational mode immediately. Borrowing a card from the British, when they'd used the BBC to broadcast orders to French resistance in World War Two, Ho used the government radio station in Saigon to spread his orders to kill over the length and breadth of South Vietnam. The key phrase was concealed in a normal daily news broadcast which was repeated several times throughout the day.

In one night, three province governors were assassinated, twenty-three village chiefs, two Ameri-

can Intelligence officers and the commander of
the *Manh Ho* Strong Tiger Ranger Battalion, one
of South Vietnam's most effective combat
elements.

Ho's losses had been minimal. Seven men and
two women killed and four taken prisoner. A very
small price to pay for the amount of fear and
disruption they had created. To Troung, Ho had
said, "We have been lucky that we have not had
more casualties, but even if it has cost twenty of
our people for everyone we killed it would be
cheap at the price. For that which we do is of more
value than the lives of two full divisions. It is
always much cheaper and quite often much easier
to kill the brains of the enemy rather than his
limbs. The losses we have inflicted on the enemy
will show dividends for a long time. Now, within
every echelon of both the civil and military
authorities, everyone will walk in constant fear."

Ho was correct in his analysis. Neither the
South Vietnamese nor the Americans trusted their
closest friends or servants. Changes were made in
trusted aides and house staffs. This did nothing to
hinder the work of the KSN. To the contrary, it
created more openings for Ho's own people to in-
filtrate.

Colonel Tomlin had all civilian Vietnamese nationals removed from the camp and would have
thrown out the ARVIN troops as well if he could
have done it without creating a political stink.
With the reports of new assassinations coming
nearly on the hour he was firmly convinced that he
was at the top of Ho's hit list even above the
Premier and General Westmoreland. All of his
clerks were issued weapons and MPs stood a

twenty-four hour guard on him. He had given up the comfort of his own villa in town and moved into the BOQ, the Bachelor Officer's Quarters, where though it was a little less than luxurious, he felt a bit safer with all the other American officers around him.

Tomlin did one thing right during this process, he appealed to the second strongest instinct in man. Greed! Through all of his Intelligence sources he had sent out the word that he would pay for information and pay well. A thousand in gold for each KSN taken dead or alive and, if desired he would arrange for that individual to be granted emigration status, which could take him to the United States. That was a prize which was almost beyond money. For the chance to escape the hell of Vietnam and thirty years of war, there were many who would have turned in their own brothers, fathers, sisters and mothers. It was a desperate ploy on Tomlin's part but he felt that no sacrifice was too great where his own safety was concerned. He managed to get the sanction of the State Department by showing the First Secretary to the Ambassador that his name was also on the list of those to be killed. The First Secretary arranged, through the Ambassador, for State Department approval of the plan. Then he and the Ambassador decided they would be of more value at this sensitive time in history if they both returned to the United States for a time. Tomlin was green with disgust at the way the cowards had run off to save their own hides. Late that night he called the Pentagon to see if a staff job offered to him six months earlier at the Army Security Agency in Maryland was still open. It wasn't.

Cursing, he applied a little pressure to get a Huey to go in and pick up the Kamserai chieftain that Romain wanted. It required a quick incursion into Cambodian territory but the Landing Zone was fairly close to the border, which was ill defined at best.

Tomlin would not take chances. If there was the remotest possibility that Romain could get to Ho, then he'd do everything in his power to see that the sergeant had his opportunity.

Casey wondered if Ho had identified him yet. He knew the Vietcong had a very good intelligence gathering vehicle. Every cleaning woman, houseboy or mechanic was a potential agent. The Americans had borrowed the colonial power's style of living. Most of those stationed in base camps had long ago come to consider the services of the Vietnamese civilians as a necessity. It was good to have someone make your bed, spit polish your boots to a high gloss and do your laundry.

Casey looked on them with disgust. How could anyone feel they had tight security with hundreds, if not thousands, of Vietnamese nationals having easy access to their installations? The rough statistic was that one out of ten was a Vietcong sympathizer and still the Americans made no effort to change the situation. It was stupid and the Americans would pay the price for their laziness.

Gomez came into the transient barracks about noon and knocked on Casey's door.

"Come in." Gomez opened the door. Casey was sitting on his bunk cleaning a Walther P-38 9 mm pistol he had conned out of a sergeant from the 173rd Airborne Brigade.

Gomez leaned up against the wall and lit up a

Winston. "Your Kamserai is on his way. He should be here in about thirty minutes. I just left Tomlin and he is in a shit fit for you to get on with things. That attempt to kill him has suddenly made him very reasonable. So get your tail up and let's go meet your friend."

Casey grunted as he rose. He put the pistol in its holster and donned his webbed belt with the P-38 hanging from his right hip. "All right, Captain, let's go. But I'd feel better if Van was with us. He knows more about the way Charlie thinks than all of us put together. But if we can't have him, then that's the way the fortune cookie crumbles."

By the time they reached the camp's chopper pad they could hear the whirling of a chopper's blades coming in from the south.

Setting down as usual in a cloud of blowing dust, leaves and small stones, the Huey cut its motor to let the blades spin down.

Phang stepped out of the side door, waved good-bye to the pilot and turned to greet his friend. Teeth as black as Chinese lacquer spread across his weathered, crinkled face as he performed what was for him a smile.

"Oho! Big Nose. It has been a long time since last we met. What is it you need of these old bones?"

Casey examined Phang. He hadn't changed much in the last twenty years. His hair had gone completely gray at the age of twenty and he had always been "the Old One" to Casey, though he probably wasn't much past his middle forties.

"It is good to see you, Old One. I'd like you to meet Captain Gomez. He's a good soldier!" Phang eyed Gomez closely then nodded his agreement. "As you say, my friend. But first take me where I can get something to drink. Flying has never been a pleasant thing for me."

Gomez shook Phang's weathered hand and led him from the chopper pad to his jeep. Once everyone was seated, he told Casey "I think it would be best if we had our drink in private. The fewer who know about your friend the better it will be."

Casey agreed and, after making a stop at the Officer's Club for whiskey, Gomez drove them over to the transient barracks where they could talk in Casey's room without much fear of interruption.

Once inside, drinks poured, toasts made and remembrances taken out, dusted and put back, they got down to business.

Casey gave him a thumbnail sketch of Colonel Ho van Tuyen and his *Ke' sat Nhan*. He didn't have to go into any details. Phang had already heard of the VC's new plan to demoralize the South Vietnamese and their allies. It was a good plan, one that he wished he could have used.

"Phang, my Old One!" Casey poured him another water glass full of Jack Daniels sour mash bourbon. "I want you to find Ho for me. He thinks that if he can kill off our brains, then our armies will fail. I think he has the right idea but the sword cuts two ways. If I kill Ho then that might disrupt his entire project and demoralize his men."

He took a pull of his own drink. Captain Gomez waited till Casey stopped speaking before he interjected, "Of course, Mr. Phang, there will be a payment made for your services. At the word "payment" Phang's eyes took on a lean and hungry look. He had an affection for money that any Wall Street broker would have appreciated.

"Now!" he chastized Casey, "there is a man who understands the reality of this world. It is not philosophy. It is money." Pointing his empty glass at Gomez he demanded to know, "How much for me and my men to do your dirty work?"

Gomez cleared his throat, suddenly a bit uncomfortable. He had never actually cleared the amount of payment Phang was to get. "I don't know, but whatever it is will be fair. Trust me!"

At the words "trust me" Phang narrowed his eyes. "Are you Jewish? You don't look Jewish." Then he burst into laughter at the old joke. Gomez just shook his head, wondering where Casey ever found a character like this. The man looked like a savage but he spoke good English and had used French expressions and expletives more than once with great fluency. Whoever he was, Phang the Old One had been around the horn a time or two.

Casey looked at Phang, winked conspiratorially and said, "I think that as the chief of the Kamserai, our good friend Phang should be given a hundred captured AK-47s and at least three RPD light machine guns, as well as a bonus payable in gold if he is successful in locating and taking me in after Comrade Ho." Phang grinned, showing his teeth like a series of shiny black tombstones.

Gomez looked a bit confused. "I don't th getting him the weapons will be a problem, why do you want captured enemy guns? We co just give him new American ones."

Casey leaned across the bunk he was sitting and took the bottle of Jack Daniels from Gome "Because, my good Captain Gomez, Phang do not like the South Vietnamese much better than he does the North. And when he needs more ammunition for his weapons I think you'll agree that it would be better if he took it from the enemy."

Gomez looked at Phang who bobbed his gray head up and down in agreement with Casey. "He is right. I will take what I need from anyone. And we all know that one day you foreigners will go home, but we will still be here."

Gomez cleared his throat and took a deep pull straight from the bottle. "I think I'll leave you two alone to discuss things while I go and see Colonel Tomlin. I do believe you have a very strong argument."

Tomlin was in a lather. Three more Vietnamese as well as two more Americans had been assassinated since the morning report. One of the American's throats had been cut by his Vietnamese wife.

He roared at Gomez. "I don't care what they want or why. Just get it for them and do it fast. Do you hear me? I know they're out there, just waiting for their chance to get me. Now get your ass out of here and give them what they want and get them the hell moving. I want Ho and his killers removed before they remove me!"

Gomez did as he was ordered. It took a couple of hours and several phone calls back and forth from several different headquarters before he had what he needed. Returning to the transient barracks, he knocked on the door before entering.

He grinned at Phang. "Well, you've got it. I'll have the weapons here in the morning, along with a couple of hundred rounds of ammo for each AK and two thousand for each light machine gun. And a radio with a preset crystal, so you'll be able to stay in constant contact with us. As for payment, I think this is fair. One thousand gold for each KSN taken dead or alive, and if you get Ho there'll be a bonus of another ten thousand."

Phang looked at Casey who nodded his head in agreement with the terms. It was a good deal. If Phang got to work he could probably make enough to finance his own country. Phang understood perfectly well what the gold would mean to him. He was, after all, a capitalist of the first water. More drinks were taken to seal the bargain. In the morning Phang would return to his people, outfit them, and send agents into the countryside to locate Comrade Ho. Once he had a fix on him he would send for Casey.

CHAPTER EIGHT

After his own near assassination, Colonel Ho had decided to move his center of operations further south. He knew that even though he was technically in an area that was off limits for the Americans they had, on occasion and when they thought the circumstances warranted it, made invasions. He was certain that they would consider him an important enough target to justify such an incursion. Besides which most of his important targets were to be found in what the South Vietnamese called Military Area III, which consisted of Saigon, Tay Ninh, Bien Hoa, Xuan Loc, Ben Cat, Vung Tau, Phouc Vinh, and Niu Bara, also known as Song Be.

He had another more personal reason for the move. From his agents he had learned that the scar-faced man was there. His pride demanded that he must punish him. Once they had made their move he would send Troung into Song Be. Troung, like himself, had good reason for wanting the American dead.

They were not three hours out of their camp and on the road south when a flight of ten Cobra helicopters struck their old camp, turning on it with miniguns and rockets. In less than five minutes Ho's former headquarters was a smoking graveyard. He saw the smoke and could hear the attack from where he and Troung sat in their American jeep at the base of a mountain junction.

Ho nudged Troung in the side, pleased that his judgment had once more been proven correct. The lives lost in the attack were of no real value. There had been only a few men in the huts, who were too ill to move and some of them worthless peasants. All those of value had already been sent out on their missions. Leaning back in his seat beside the driver, he looked back at Troung sitting in the rear. "We fooled them again, didn't we?" Troung agreed, but worry ticked at the edge of his eyes. He had an uneasy feeling about the future.

Ho was in good spirits for the trip south to his new *Bo-chi-huy,* his new headquarters, in the place called the Parrot's Beak near Rieng in Cambodia. The region, though claimed by Cambodia, was totally controlled by the Vietcong who were the de facto masters of the region.

Colonel Tomlin was not pleased at the report forwarded to him from the Cobra flight leader. He grumbled to Gomez, "It appears that our protagonist anticipated our gambit and has already moved out."

Gomez requested permission to smoke, was given it and after lighting up asked, "Why do you say that, sir?"

Tomlin showed him the after action report. "Because there was not enough resistance to indicate any kind of a main force installation there. The Cobras only received a small amount of return fire, and it was all small arms. On the ground they saw very few of the enemy. If Colonel Ho had still been in residence, the enemy response would certainly have been much more violent. No! The son of a bitch has taken off and he's not going back. Pass the word on to Sergeant Romain and his Kamserai. It is my opinion that Ho is moving south to be closer to the center of things. He'll probably set up shop in the Parrot's Beak. It's the most secure area for him. I would if I were in his place."

It made sense to Gomez and he did as he was ordered. He had a regular time set for Phang to check in and would pass on the information he'd received from Tomlin to him.

Phang immediately sent out several groups of his men to the Parrots Beak. They had to travel on foot and it would take at least four days for them to get there. If Ho had moved in, his men should be able to find out from the local peasants. In Cambodia the situation would be reversed for the Vietcong. They were the enemy and the population was not in sympathy with their foreign masters.

It was ten days before Phang reported back to Gomez.

Gomez located Casey at the "Club New York" in town. Pulling a chair over to where he could share the breeze from a roof fan, he ordered a Bamiba beer and waited till the bar girl was out of earshot before talking.

"Phang checked in. His people have located our boy. He's in the Parrot's Beak, a little east of Rieng and not twenty minutes by chopper from Tay Ninh. He has a one-handed man with him. That's probably your friend, Captain Troung. If they're that close you can bet your ass that things are going to start getting hot around here."

Casey sipped his own beer and nodded, brushing away a bothersome fly. "All right! So Phang has him located. I want you to arrange a reconnaissance flight over the site and get me some pictures. But don't be too obvious about it. We don't want to spook them again."

Gomez finished his beer and was getting up to leave when Casey stopped him with one more request. "Captain, I think that we should consider going in after him. Tell Phang to get ready. I want him to take his men and move as close as he can to Ho's camp without being spotted. Depending on what the reconnaissance flight shows, we may be able to go in and take him. I prefer that to letting him make all the moves."

Gomez looked down at Casey. "You do know that if you go into Cambodia you'll be on your own and we can do nothing to help you if you get caught. It's one thing to send in some choppers to shoot the place up, but if you're on the ground you'll have to take care of yourself. Our leaders, in their infinite wisdom, do not yet let us cross into privileged sanctuaries, especially the Parrot's Beak. At my last briefing we learned that there are at least four full hard-core PAVN and Vietcong regiments in permanent residence there, and probably a lot more that we don't know about. If we were to try and get in there it'd take a major ground force operation and that is not likely to be approved in the foreseeable future."

Casey looked up, straight into Gomez's eyes, "I don't care!" He went back to his beer.

Gomez gave a shudder. He didn't envy Ho having this man on his ass. He had the distinct impression that Casey would go after Ho if he was in the presidential palace in Hanoi. Well, his was not to reason why. Tomlin had told him to give Casey what he wanted and that's what he would do.

During the next few days, Casey had Gomez bring him every map he could get his hands on showing the area around Rieng, It was mostly flat, with plantations of rubber trees and palms covering a good portion of the region. Rice fields and heavy patches of woods made up the rest. It took three days for a reconnaissance flight to be made by a Thai civilian DC-4 airline flying the regular route from Saigon to Phnom Penh. The plane was rerouted a few miles off of its normal flight path in order to pass over the target area. It had been equipped with special cameras which could show the size of a zit on a Charlie's nose at ten thousand feet.

Studying the photographs with the aid of a magnifying glass Casey and Gomez mapped it out. The new site of Comrade Ho's operation was located in a Cambodian village where the civilians were kept in residence, probably to keep the Americans from making an air strike on it if they got too pissed off. They'd have to kill neutrals to get to the VC, something the American politicians were not likely to sanction. Under the magnifying glass they located several places that looked like tunnel openings. Charlie was so confident of his safety that he'd gotten a little careless. One shot showed two men lowering a crate into a hole by a hayrick. That probably meant that Ho had his headquarters underground, with the village directly overhead. From what they could tell it looked as if there were at least two full companies assigned to the village's defense. Under normal circumstances that would probably have been sufficient, as any American ground force would have to advance through at least a full regiment to get there, giving Ho plenty of time in which to move out again.

Phang radioed that he was one night's march from Ho, and was ready to move on an instant's notice. He had eighty men with him, all good fighters, who had proven themselves more than once. Casey told Gomez to tell Phang to stay put. He had to come up with a way to get in and out. If they stayed in the village too long, they'd be cut off by the other VC units in the area. They'd have to get in and get out fast.

He and Gomez went over a dozen different options, none of them acceptable. Casey needed an ally, and it was given to him by the meteorology people on Formosa and Luzon. He had a friend coming in and he would be here in three days.

Gomez wasn't terribly fond of the idea Casey finally brought to him, but he had to admit he had nothing better to offer. If that was what he wanted, then that's what he'd get.

Captain Troung was pleased. Ho had given him permission to send two of his men into Song Be with a new target, the scar-faced one. He had been positively identified. When they'd reached the new camp, photos of the man were waiting for him. Two of them showed him in the company of an American captain who worked for a Colonel Tomlin. The KSN agents were already in Song Be, waiting for an opportunity to kill the man. They were perfectly ready to die in the process if it meant success.

•   •   •

Casey had done all that he could. He'd be ready
to go in two days. All that he was waiting for was
a special piece of gear that had to be sent up to
him from Saigon, and the man who could okay it
was on R&R in Hong Kong and wouldn't be back
for another day. Casey went into town to get rid
of some of the tension that had been building in
him for the last couple of weeks. Idleness had
always driven him crazy, but there wasn't anything he could do about it until he got in the equip-
ment and information he needed.

Song Be was like most cities its size—houses
with tin roofs, slums where families lived ten to a
room and children played in drainage ditches that
were overrun with filth. The more wealthy mer-
chants had villas in the French style, where they
lived behind whitewashed walls with broken glass
cemented in on the tops of the walls to keep out
their poorer, more desperate countrymen. One
section of the town was set aside for Americans to
party in and was patrolled by both US and South
Vietnamese Military Police. That was where he
was going, back to the "Club New York." Club
New York? That was a laugh. The only thing that
remotely resembled New York was the name. It
wasn't too pretty, much the same as any of the
others on the strip. A bar with a tile floor, where
GI's danced with attractive Vietnamese girls who
would play five-hundred rummy for a drink or for
love. A narrow porch ran along the front but it
wasn't used much at night. It was too easy for a
grenade to be tossed in, or a machine gun to spray
the drinkers from the back of a motorcycle or cab.
The rest of the bar front had a strong wire screen

over the windows to protect the customers from their cousins.

Casey didn't notice the two pairs of eyes that watched him enter the bar. Ngo vinh Long and Pham Dong had been waiting patiently for him to come again to the bar. Ngo had a small pushcart from which he sold ice cream bars to the GIs and bar girls. Pham Dong worked for another bar across the street, the "Club Paradise," which was even seedier than the New York. He stood at the door to entice drunk GIs in to sample the whiskey and the girls. He was quite good at it and made several large tips.

Both were eager to finish their assignment. They didn't know why their leaders wanted this lowly sergeant killed, but the importance of their succeeding had been emphasized to them. The scarfaced man must die, even if they had to give up their lives in the process. Ngo and Pham Dong had talked about just walking up to him, pulling the pins on a couple of hand grenades and holding on to him till they exploded. That plan was scrapped because the man looked to be very strong and he might be able to break loose from them.

After lengthy contemplation and analysis of their options they decided they would do their job in a more trustworthy manner, which would also give them a better chance at survival. They were ready to die, but not if they didn't have to.

CHAPTER NINE

Inside, the New York was the usual mixture: chopper pilots and their crews, tanker commanders and their crews, and even some of the Special Forces men from the B Team at Song Be. They had their crew too. Segregation had reached a new level of meaning. Oriental girls wearing western makeup tried to look like what they thought American girls should. They carefully studied *Cosmopolitan* and *Glamour* magazines in their rooms and tried to mimic the openmouthed expressions of high fashion models and actresses. To Casey's thinking they would have been much better off to have remained themselves rather than trying to become clones.

By midnight the club would be empty. Curfew was on. Casey stayed to himself; he was not part of any group and didn't want to be. This was not a night to drink and whore. He was just getting cabin fever from hanging around headquarters all day. A few beers then back to the transient barracks.

The atmosphere in the New York became too heavy with bullshit. He paid his tab, ignored the offer in the barmaid's eyes and left.

He checked his watch. It was only 2030 hours. On the mud and cobblestone streets GIs moved in twos and threes. Only a fool went out to drink or get laid by himself. In most of the groups there was at least one man who stayed sober to watch over his friends. The next time out on the town someone else would do the job. That man probably had a pistol stuck in his belt or in a shoulder holster. Weapons were not supposed to be taken off post when on pass but the order was generally ignored and no one tried with any real effort to enforce it.

Through habit, Casey scanned the street. Taking his time he watched the men and women, not really looking for anything but expecting everything. It was a good policy to always check for anything that was unnatural. The way a man or woman moved, the expression in the eyes of a street beggar or bartender. The night was fairly slow. Not too many on the streets. He thought for a moment about getting an ice cream from the man with the pushcart. But the Vietnamese liked theirs the same way the French did. Too sweet. He decided to pass. He lit up a smoke and headed back to camp.

Most of the lights on the streets came from the bars and shops that catered to the GIs. At intersections there were a few street lights to keep the streets from being in total darkness, but these only lit up the immediate area. Moths and flies gathered around the hazy globes of brilliance in humming swarms. Casey moved away from the strip. Passing into the darker streets, he didn't notice that he had an escort bringing up drag. Ngo and Pham Dong left their jobs and tailed after their target, one on each side of the street. Under their loose jackets each carried a pistol with a round in the chamber. Once out of sight of the strip with its wandering patrols of military police, they would pick a place, get their prey between them and cut him down.

They kept to the shadows on the sides of the streets, stopping to look in shop windows and each playing the role of one who was only out wandering the streets, perhaps because the night was too hot and heavy to get any sleep.

Casey stopped at a street vendor to buy a pack of American Winstons and looked over the other selections the turbaned Tonkinese had to offer. Cans of Folgers coffee, a Sony radio and cans of evaporated milk were what he was building his future on. If it hadn't been for the black market supporting them, tens of thousands of Vietnamese would have had no jobs at all.

He moved on, this time turning off the main streets to a narrow alley where there were no lights at all. Here, between the main streets everything was in blackness. Only a few thin glows from kerosene lamps broke through dirty windows where men and women huddled on straw mats with their families to wait for the dawn. He could smell the humanity packed in close together. The odors of fish and charcoal mixed with the sourness of urine and honey buckets used to collect each families' night soil.

He lit up a fresh smoke and made one more turn to the left, passing a chopping block where meat was prepared during the day and the entrails of slaughtered goats, hogs and dogs were tossed to the rats which ran the fences and alleys as cats do in western cities.

Ngo and Pham Dong wondered what he was

doing. True, this route was a bit shorter, but it was off the path normally taken by Americans to get back to their installation. Had they been spotted? Or had he just taken a wrong turn? Now, in the dark, all they could see of him was the burning end of his cigarette. It was a beacon they had to follow. Once they reached the chopping block they had to come close together.

Where was he? He had disappeared. Pistols in their hands, they tried to see through the darkness. Pham Dong nudged Ngo and pointed with his pistol to a narrow passage between two houses. There they could see the red glow of a cigarette. So that was it! The American was trying to lure them in to where he could get at them. Pham Dong thought *Xin Loi, GI*. But he wasn't really sorry.

He and Ngo moved a bit away from each other, eyes straining to pierce the darkness. They could barely make out an outline with the lit end of the cigarette set head high. Was the man a fool or was he drunk? He didn't seem to be drunk, but then who cared. They had him! The space between the houses went nowhere. He was in a cul-de-sac.

Both men raised their weapons. Fingers squeezed and the night exploded with the crack of their pistol shots as they pumped every round in the magazines into the shadowed outline. They were very cool, placing their shots just below the glow of the cigarette. The smell of cordite mingled with those of the street as they ceased firing.

What was going on? The shadow didn't move. It just stood there with the cigarette still burning. They were still trying to figure it out when Casey rose up from behind the chopping block. Not

wasting any time he shot each of them once in the
back of the head. The 9 mm bullets from his P-38
were the exploding types with mercury cores. The
two men's heads looked as if they were ripe grapes
placed between the fingers of a strong man and
then popped. Their skulls simply exploded; rup-
tured brains and bone fragments spewed out the
front of their faces.

Stepping over the bodies, Casey went to the
shadowy figure the VC had emptied their pistols
into. He took his cigarette from between the fibers
of the rolled up straw mat and took a deep drag.
From a block away he could hear whistles starting
to blow as MPs tried to figure out where the shots
had come from. Quickly he checked the bodies for
papers. There were none, only a few dollars worth
of piasters. He took these and the two pistols with
him and left the corpses for the cat-sized street rats
to nibble on.

He looked to the sky. Heat lightning flickered in
the heavens. A false promise of rain that wouldn't
come this night. Casey was tired but also relieved.
At last something had happened. He knew they
were not just a couple of would-be thieves or part-
time guerrillas who saw him as an easy mark. They
had to have come from Comrade Ho, and that
was good. The way it should be.

The MPs at the gate waved him in. They had
been the same ones on duty when he'd left the
camp. They wondered why he was back so early.
Probably too broke to get any action.

It felt good that night to crawl between clean
sheets and close his eyes. He'd get his special gear
in the morning and be on his way to join Phang

the next day. He wondered how well Ho and Troung were resting?

After a morning chow of powdered eggs and Australian bacon he returned to the transient barracks. He picked up the two pistols he'd taken off the dead Charlies and went to see Gomez, who was at his desk having his breakfast in the form of five cups of coffee. The captain hadn't been able to sleep, wondering what the events of the next few days would bring.

Tossing the two guns on Gomez's desk he asked, "I guess you've heard about the two Viets who were killed last night?"

Gomez picked the pieces up, checked the chambers and magazines on each of them, then placed them slowly back on his desk. "Would you like to tell me about it? Or should I just pretend this never happened?"

Casey sat down in the metal straight-backed, gray-painted chair across from Gomez. "They were from our good friend, Comrade Ho. He knows who I am and where I am. I wouldn't be surprised if he knows about you too. If he's after me, then it's also possible that by our recent association you may be on his hit list now. If I were you, Captain, I think I would be very careful for a while."

Gomez's response was drowned out by a flight of Cobras passing overhead, probably on their way to Vung Tau where they would be in support of an Air Cavalry, Search and Destroy operation in the "Special War Zone" near the Parrot's Beak.

Gomez looked up at the ceiling with ill-disguised irritation until the choppers faded away.

"I said, you certainly have a way of making a day start off like shit!"

Casey grinned, the scar on his face folding into a wrinkle as he did. He liked the Mexican-American. A good man, as he'd thought earlier. He was tough, like the old Spaniards of Castile.

Pouring a cup of coffee for himself from Gomez's overworked coffee pot, he asked, "Have you heard from our man in Saigon? I need that gear and I need it today so I can check it over before taking off tomorrow. By the way, what time is the flight laid on for, and have you decided whether it would be best if we go in for a landing or do I jump?"

Gomez swallowed half a cup and grimaced. He was on the verge of a caffeine high. "The items you requested will be here by noon and you'll be jumping. It will be harder that way for any Charlies to locate you than if the chopper set down somewhere. You've jumped from heli-copters before haven't you?"

Casey nodded as he refused Gomez's offer to refill his cup. "Yeah, I've jumped from them a few times. No problem. Have you set up the drop zone with Phang?"

Gomez replied a bit testily, "Don't you think that anyone else can do their job? Of course it's set up and if I have any luck at all the wind will blow you right into the center of a VC staging area, where you'll finally have something else to do other than bug me!"

Casey smiled easily as he got up to leave. "I'll be in the barracks. Send someone to get me when my gear comes in. In the meantime you should lay off that poison you call coffee and take up something safe, like arsenic.''

It was a little after 1300 hours when a PFC came to fetch Casey back to Gomez's office.

''Here's your gear. Check it over and see if it's everything you need.''

Casey opened up the gray-blue flight bag, checked out each article and zipped it back up. ''It's all there. I'll need to borrow a jeep to go out to where I can test them in private. We don't need any audience.''

Gomez gave him his own jeep with a cautious warning. ''You be careful with that damned thing. It took me six months to get one of my own, and don't you let anything happen to it.''

While Casey was in the field testing his new acquisitions, Dai Uy Troung was meeting with his superior officer. Ducking his head to avoid a low beam, Troung passed several guards in the tunnel passage leading to Ho's subterranean office.

Announcing himself he forgot to lower his head and bumped it against a palm tree beam above the doorway as he entered the office. Without stopping work on the letter he was drafting to Hanoi, Ho laughed at his aide's accident. ''If that gives you a headache I have some aspirin in my desk.''

Troung rubbed his head with his one hand. ''I think that we may both have a headache, sir.''

Ho stopped what he was doing. ''What do you mean?''

Troung took a paper from the pocket of his black cotton shirt. ''This has just come in. It was received by radio this morning. The two men we sent to kill the one named Romain have failed. They are both dead. Their heads were blown off.''

Ho's face developed a worried expression.

"Comrade Troung. I have just had a most strange feeling. It was as if the scar-faced one was watching us, looking at us as though we were dead. I must have *him* dead. There is something about him that means nothing but evil for us as long as he is alive. You know that some people's lives are intertwined from the moment they meet? That is what I feel has happened with him. The only way to break the connection is by death, either his or ours. Come to me with a new plan by the day after tomorrow."

Troung said nothing, only bowed in acceptance of his master's orders, orders he completely concurred with. He would find a way to put an end to their enemy. An enemy that had become a very personal threat. Sergeant Romain had to die.

CHAPTER TEN

It was time. Gomez took Casey to the chopper pad. One of the older Hueys stood throbbing on the perforated steel-plated deck. It only carried the pilot, a lieutenant, and a warrant officer co-pilot. Casey climbed inside and Gomez handed him up his gear, including a bag with his parachute inside. He'd harness up after they were airborne. He didn't want to give any eyes that weren't friendly any idea that he was going to make a jump somewhere. Having only the pilot and copilot on board was another false indicator that this was not a flight heading for any action. If it had been, there would have been two door gunners sitting behind M-60s.

Gomez moved away from the slow spinning blades and waved a hand in farewell. He had to cover his eyes as the blades picked up speed, for an instant turning the pad into a miniature tornado.

Casey fastened the seat belt holding him to the red canvas seats as the Huey tilted its nose slightly downward, lifted up from the ass end and moved away from the pad. The flight wouldn't take very long, less than an hour to the drop zone. As the chopper rose to a safer altitude, he leaned out of the open door to look down at the earth below. Terraced fields of rice lay in neat squares like

those on a patchwork quilt. Song Be didn't even
look clean from the air as they moved away from
the warrens of tin roofs and shacks. They were
following the sun. Here, where the land was low
and flat, it took longer to set. The chopper sped
on. It felt good in the sky, cleaner somehow.
Maybe it was the wind blowing through the open
side doors that made it seem so. Anyway it felt
good. He could understand why pilots were so
reluctant to do ground duty.

By the time they reached the Cambodian border
the sun was nearly down. The fields below had
given way to rubber plantations. Fields of sugar-
cane interspersed with heavy patches of tropical
forest. The greens of the fields and jungle changed
to strange mixtures of blood orange and emerald
as the sun set at the edge of the world. Its light
lingered on for a few minutes more, then it was
gone. The air grew chiller as Casey opened his bag
and put on his chute, taking his time to adjust the
straps snugly and still keep his family jewels out of
the way. He had no reserve chute; he'd be jumping
at five-hundred feet. At that altitude there
wouldn't be time for a reserve to open anyway.
The rest of his gear was strapped onto the D rings
that normally held the reserve.

Spotted around on the dark earth below them
were pricks of light from campfires, where villagers made their homes near their fields and or-
chards. Some of those fires probably belonged to
Charlie, but now that they were in Cambodian
airspace the Vietcong wouldn't be too concerned
about being hit.

The pilot turned on the warning light and yelled
back, "You've got five minutes to the drop zone.

We're descending now, so get your ass ready." Casey hooked up his static line and moved to sit in the doorway, his feet dangling out over the darkness, ears deafened by the rush of wind and heavy throbbing of the chopper's blades.

Phang had his men spread out around the clearing. Some had been placed at ambush sites on the trails leading in to the DZ. Four of his men had flashlights. They formed a cross in the clearing. When they heard the Huey, they turned on the lights to guide it in.

Casey's other ally was on its way to join them. A typhoon, born in the Sulu Sea, had crossed over Palawan Island and was now off the coast of Vietnam in the South China Sea, bringing torrential rains and winds of a hundred and sixty miles an hour. There was nothing to slow it down before it hit land. On the coastal regions storm warnings had already been sent out. As for those further inland, many didn't even know the storm was on its way. The typhoon would lose much of its punch as it moved inland, but the winds should still be around eighty miles an hour when it reached Cambodia.

Casey's greatest concern was that the typhoon might change course. If it did then the job would be three times as tough to do.

The Huey flew with all of its lights off. The interior of the chopper was lit only by the dim red glow necessary to see the instrument panels. The pilot spoke to Casey for the second time. "There it is."

Leaning forward out of the door to look ahead, Casey saw the thin tubes of light forming a cross on the black earth, marking the perimeter of the drop zone. He yelled back to the pilot. "Let's do it then!"

At five-hundred feet the Huey slowed to a crawl, then hovered for ten seconds. It gave a sudden lurch upward as two-hundred pounds left it. Without waiting to see if Casey got down okay the pilot moved the Huey on. He'd go straight in for another twenty miles then make a circle, taking him back to Song Be.

To exit the Huey all Casey had to do was lean forward till he fell out of the door. Then he was jerked up as the static pulled the chute out of its bag. The opening shock was, as always, welcome. He didn't have time to think about it much. At five-hundred feet he'd only be in the air twenty seconds before hitting the deck. It was pitch black. Once he'd jumped, the flashlights on the ground went out. He went into the landing position, chin tucked against his chest, toes down, legs slightly bent. He tried to see the tree line as he fell to give him some idea of how far he was from the ground, but it was too dark to even do that. He just had to wait for it. He hit, automatically going into a toes, hip, thigh roll that brought him back on to his feet, his hands hitting the quick release on his chest to free him from the harness. His chute was already being collapsed by the willing hands of Phang's Kamserai. They leaped on it to take the air out. Before he was out of his harness, his chute was already being rolled up and taken off the drop zone to be buried.

Phang rushed to help him with his gear. Casey checked the action on the M-3 .45 submachine gun. After making sure it worked, he responded to Phang's greetings.

"It's good to see you again, Old One. But I don't think we should stay here to visit." Phang grunted, a bit irritated at his friend's cursory welcome. But then all Big Noses were that way.

Leaving the drop zone behind, they faded into the dark traveling in single file, with flankers out a hundred meters to their right and left, and a point man another fifty up to the front. Casey stayed to the center with Phang in front of him. All of a sudden the night became very close, very heavy, after the coolness of the ride in the Huey. Following a narrow trail between fields and small groups of rubber trees and plantains, they marched three hours till they reached the area Phang had selected as their base camp.

Phang was a cautious old bird. He had chosen a site in a grove of wild plantains right next to a leper colony. The VC avoided the lepers as if they had the plague. It would be as safe here as anywhere.

Late that night, he and the Kamserai chieftain went over the plans. Phang had been concerned about their chances of success until he'd found out about the typhoon. He knew something was happening because of the stillness of the air. Like many of the jungle animals, Phang had many of the instincts common to the so-called primitive peoples of the world who lived closer to nature. He had known that a storm was coming; he just didn't know how big it was going to be. Once he knew that, it didn't take him long to figure out the rest. The hardest part of the operation would be getting in through the initial defenses surrounding the village. They had till the next night to wig that out. It was Phang who came up with part of the answer. He would get some of his people inside the village before nightfall.

Troung and Ho also knew that a storm was coming. They listened to the weather reports on Radio Saigon. Their own *Giai Phong* (Liberation Radio) weather information was not kept much up to date. The broadcasts from Saigon were much more accurate. As for storm damage, they weren't that concerned. Most of their important facilities and supply depots were underground. There would be a bit of flooding, naturally, and some temporary interruption of communication, but nothing they couldn't deal with. The storms were always much more damaging to the enemy than to them. What was the saying the Americans used? It is an ill wind that blows no good? If it was a good wind it would destroy many enemy aircraft while on the ground.

With dawn came the first light winds, a touch of rain riding with them. Nothing threatening about them. Instead it made the day much cooler and pleasant, but Casey knew that would quickly change before night fell, when the winds would rise to an ear shattering crescendo that would bring death and destruction for hundreds of square miles.

Phang sent five of his men into the village. Dressed as peasants, they carried no weapons with them in their baskets filled with breadfruit, mangoes and plantains. Phang had met with some of the villagers who had come out to see that their goats and water buffaloes were taken care of. To the villagers he had said only that he wished for his men to be let into the village where they could get information on the Vietnamese there and report back to the Cambodian government in Phnom Penh. The villagers figured they had nothing to lose if the government was wanting information about the Vietcong. Perhaps that meant they were getting ready to do something to get rid of them. That was a situation to be desired.

The storm hit the Vietnamese coast, bringing tides fifteen-feet above normal and winds that tore apart straw and board houses as though they were made of paper. It rode across the delta behind a front of black clouds filled with moisture gathered up in the South China Sea.

Phang went over the layout of the village with Casey. It was a rectangle with a rim of trees running all the way around it. It was in the trees that the first line of defense waited. Hidden by the trees out of sight of the air were a line of bunkers and a single apron of barbed wire. In the wire were an unknown number of claymore mines and other booby traps, as well as a field of punji stakes. Not terribly formidable for a well armed and equipped American battalion to take, but it was enough that, if they weren't careful, it could mean the deaths of many of Phang's men.

In Casey's bag were what he hoped would be the easy way in now that Phang had some of his men inside the village. Once the main group of Kamserai made it inside, they'd head for entrances to the underground network. That was where the shit could get very heavy.

Vietcong and PAVN troops were preparing for the onslaught of the storm, taking shelter. They had experienced typhoons before and knew it would be a long night, a very wet and unpleasant night. The winds were increasing, now up to nearly fifty miles an hour as the VC tied down and got ready.

Casey and Phang used this time to move into assault positions, just out of sight of the first line of the village's defenses. There they would wait till the storm was at its peak.

The night came early; the skies darkened and rumbled. Lightning broke through the clouds to crack and thunder over the earth, drowning out all sounds. Lines began to go down between the different Vietcong posts. The Viets couldn't know that many of them were cut by the Kams. Radio and ground line communication was nearly nil throughout the entire Parrot's Beak. Even if a call for help got through it would take the enemy a long time to respond and for them to make their way through the winds to give any support.

Trees began to give way. The shallow roots of palms were being torn out of the earth to fall, and in some cases to be thrown, as much as a quarter of a mile before crashing into the sides of houses. Anyone that could took shelter. Facing the storm from their bunkers the Viets on duty kept their faces away from the firing apertures to avoid the cutting wind and rain. They hunched down to wait it out, wet and miserable as the waters began to fill the floor of the bunkers.

In the tunnels below water also came in, but not as much as might have been expected. All the entrances were well covered and protected. There were also conduits for drainage of the tunnels as the village sat on a small flat rise. It was drier underground than on the surface. Even the sounds of the thunder lessened to only distant rumbles. Troung and Ho felt secure.

Phang's men in the camp moved out. It was time. On their bellies they crawled to the bunker on the southeast corner. Nearly invisible under the sheet of rain and darkness, they crawled face to foot. When they reached the opening to the machine gun bunker they took out the weapons they had borrowed from the villagers, *cai kiem*, homemade swordlike machetes. They had nearly been born with one of these in their hands.

They waited till all five of them were at the entrance and ready. When the next roll of thunder came over the village, they moved. Sliding into the bunker entrance on their bellies, they slithered over the slick mud like serpents, one after the other. The three Vietnamese in the bunker raised their heads in the dark to see who it was that had joined them. They'd raised their heads just in time to meet the swinging blades of the *cai kiems* in the Kamserai warriors' hands. They died. Their screams, carried away by the wind, went unheard by any one over ten feet away.

One of the Kamserai went back outside the bunker. In his hand he carried a round object. Climbing to the top of the bunker, he raised his arm, and fighting the wind threw the object over the wire to land in a drainage ditch. The object was picked up and brought to Phang by a smiling warrior. Grabbing it by the hair, Phang held the severed head of a Vietcong up for Casey to look at. They had the bunker!

Casey nodded. It was nearly useless to try and speak over the screaming of the winds. Taking his bag he moved to the wire, raised his arm and heaved as hard as he could. The wind aided him as it was coming from his rear. The bag flew over the bunker to land four feet behind it, where it was retrieved and taken inside.

Three of the Kamserai warriors exchanged their clothes with those of the dead Viets. The blood would not show up at night and their uniforms would be washed clean by the rain before they traveled ten feet. From the bags they took out what Casey had thrown to them. Two more 45 caliber grease guns and for each of the weapons there was, in a leather foam padded case, a silencer.

The Kamserai moved out of the bunker, going down the line to the main gate. There they would have to take out two machine gun emplacements, one on each side of the gate. Once that was done, Phang and Casey would be able to take their men and rush the camp without having to cross the mine and punji stake field.

One man went to each bunker and entered. He was made welcome as his uniform was recognized by the occupants. The heavy subsonic 45 caliber slugs tore them apart. Outside, the other two Kams stood watch, each with an AK-47 they'd taken from the Viets they'd killed in the first bunker. Once those waiting outside the wire were given the "all clear," they went for the gate.

CHAPTER ELEVEN

Under cover of the storm, Phang's men struggled to the main gate. The wind and rain tried to whip them away then switched its direction to try and force them onto the barbed wire. The typhoon was at its peak nearing winds of approximately eighty miles an hour. Wire cutters opened gaps in the barbed wire where men could slip through. It was done as much by touch as by sight, which came only in the brief, eye blinking flashes of lightning.

On the opposite side of the camp several land mines went off as tree branches were blown into the fields. The sound was barely audible, the wind a roaring monstrous vacuum cleaner sucking all sound away. The Viets inside the bunkers didn't think anything of it. It had happened before, and if it had been an attack, those on duty would have opened fire and sent up flares to warn the rest of the camp. It was a good thing that that was the way they thought.

Phang's first casualty came while trying to get through the gap in the gate wire. A Kam's assault rifle caught a thin wire on its sight. The mine went off, killing him and wounding two more. It also opened up the rest of the wire to let them into the village. Phang's men had no more trouble and left the Kamserai mercenary where he died, using his

93

body as a bridge to cross over a barrier of tangle-foot.

Phang's Kamserai did as they'd been instructed. They split up into two groups each going with one of the men with the silenced grease guns. They were to take out one at a time all the other Viets along the defense perimeter. Once they had eliminated the surface defense, they were to place men wearing VC uniforms at each entrance to the underground network. Any VC that came out would die, thinking it was one of his own men helping him.

Taking ten Kams with them, Casey and Phang headed for one of the entrances to the underground world of Comrade Ho.

They slipped and slid, pushed and pummeled by blasting winds as they crawled through foaming pools of water. Their clothes stuck to them like second skins. A wide shallow river now ran through the center of the village. In their houses, the Cambodians huddled together and prayed for the night to end. They had no interest in what was going on outside, and if they had looked out and seen Phang's men killing the Viets they would have said and done nothing other than shrug their shoulders and hope it was for the best.

Casey pulled back the canvas and thatch covering over a hole leading down into the earth. Dropping in, he was followed by a small waterfall of rich brown fluid. Phang came in behind him, then another ten of his best men, all specially chosen for this job of rat catching under the earth.

At the entrance to the passageway Casey was in, a man nearly had to go to his knees in order to move. Half squatting, he duck walked forward, the long silenced snout of the grease gun in front of him, the bolt pulled back, ready to fire. The passageway continued in a straight direction for about forty-feet before it widened out and the roof was high enough to stand in. The tunnels had been built to last, with strong beams shoring up the sides and ceiling. Mats of woven rice straw were placed between the beams to keep the worst of the drainage down to bearable levels.

At the place where the tunnel widened Casey saw a light from a lantern. He slowed and signaled to Phang to keep his men quiet. Dropping to his belly he snaked forward till he could get a look. By the lantern sat three Viets at a small half-sized table made of old ammo crates. One was asleep, his head on his arms, his weapon leaning up against the side of the tunnel. The other two talked while they smoked Vietnamese cigarettes which gave off an acrid yellow smoke.

Casey waited, listening to see if there was anyone else close by. He heard nothing but the faintest roar of the winds above and the trickle of water seeping through the roof to drop in small puddles on the floor of the tunnel. He sighted, took his time and fired. The silencer made strange whooshing, popping sounds as the bolt moved back and forth. Casey put out a ten round burst just to make sure. The three men were dead. The one sleeping with his head on his arms never woke up in time to die. He was blown off his stool to lie up against the wall next to his rifle, much the same as he had been while asleep, except that now he had no left side to his head. Phang moved past Casey. The room the three Charlies were in was a junction where two other tunnels took off in dif-

ferent directions. Casey took the nearest one on
his right and sidestepped keeping his back against
the wall till he was at the next opening. Peeking
around the corner he made a low whistle to attract
Phang's attention and motioned him over. Phang
took a look. It was a barracks. Rows of low single
bunks with straw mattresses ran along each side of
the room. Exactly twenty-two of them. There was
a weapons rack near the opposite exit filled with
AK-47s and SKS assault rifles. Each of the bunks
had an occupant and they were all asleep.

Phang nodded at Casey that he knew what had
to be done. Turning his head, he whispered something to the first man in line behind him, who
passed it on to the last. Casey moved into the barracks as quietly as possible, passing the sleeping
rows of men till he reached the other end. Looking
down the corridor he could see nothing. Only a
single coal oil lamp provided illumination for the
tunnel. Going back into the barracks, Casey stood
beside the bunk of the Viet sleeping nearest the
exit. He leaned over and swung his fist. The Viet
would not wake up until what was about to happen was over. Pointing to the next bunk and then
to himself, he motioned back to Phang to get on
with it.

Phang's ten Kams moved to where each of them
stood between two sleeping Viets. In their hands
they held their traditional machete swords raised
above the heads of the Viets. They waited. Phang
raised his hand then let it drop. The blades fell.
Each man put all the strength in his arms and
shoulders into his swing. At the same moment ten
Viets died in their sleep as Kamserai steel severed
their heads from their bodies. As if it had been

choreographed for a team of professional dancers, the ten Kams turned in unison and swung again on the opposite side of them. Once more ten blades fell and twenty Viets went to join the spirits of their ancestors. Casey killed his other man at the same time the Kams took out their first ten. He didn't have a machete, but a bayonet plunged through the thin bone of the temple worked just as well.

Phang sent his men to guard the entrances to the barracks. Casey had some work to do. The one survivor was slapped back into consciousness. A hand clamped over his mouth as he jerked back into awareness, eyes wild and frightened at the wet, dripping men with bloody blades in their hands, moving among the decapitated ruins of his comrades. They were nearly as terrifying as the visage of the scarred one, whose hand nearly crushed his face. Phang put his own dark face close to that of their prisoner.

"Where is Ho's quarters? Tell me the truth and you live. Lie, or make any outcry, and you join your friends."

The Viet slowly raised a hand to point down the hallway that Casey had looked down earlier. He removed his hand to permit the man to speak. The Viet made no attempt to cry out a warning. The feel of Phang's steel against his throat made it difficult enough to even croak out a whisper.

"The Colonel stays down this hall to the right. The third door." Phang prompted him for more information. "There are guards there, at least two, and more men in the rooms next to him. Mostly officers." The point of the blade pressed a bit deeper drawing a single pearl of blood from the

Viet's neck. "I swear it. He is there now!"

Casey nodded. He believed the man was telling the truth. He swung his fist again, putting the Viet back to sleep. He usually tried to keep his end of a bargain.

On the surface above, Phang's men had finished their mission. The bodies of the dead VC had been stripped and weapons taken from them. A team of ten Kamserai left the camp, taking with them captured weapons and ammunition. If anything went wrong they would not leave the camp empty-handed and weapons were more valuable than gold, for they meant life.

The rest took up positions and waited in the rain. Some lay under the shelter of animal pens, where they shared their accommodations with pigs and goats who snuffed at them but finally left them alone. They didn't like the smell of death and blood on the men. Others found the fuel supply for the camp under the cover of a palm-thatched hut. Grunting and slipping in the slick mud of the village compound, they rolled the drums of gasoline out of the hut and over to where they would be needed later.

Casey took the lead again. Now it was time to go after Comrade Ho. They had been lucky so far and it was not a time for mistakes. The last Kam out of the barracks stopped and looked at the only surviving Viet, shrugged his shoulders and slit the unconscious man's throat. It was stupid to leave an enemy alive, no matter what he was promised!

Casey was nearly to Ho's doorway when their luck changed. At the far end of the tunnel three VC came around a corner. They were going to the mess hall two corridors over to get something to eat before relieving the radio man and the arms room guard. Two of them had their weapons slung on their shoulders. The other carried his semiautomatic SKS in his hand. As luck would have it, he was the end man. Casey cut the first two down with the M-3. The last Viet ducked back behind the corner and began to call out the alarm.

His cries for help reached several ears. Men began to tumble from bunks, grabbing their weapons. He jacked a round into the chamber of his assault rifle and without looking around the corner, stuck the weapon out and began to fire blind. Casey was already on his belly, a grenade in his hand. Two rounds from the wild firing Charlie hit one Kam in the face. Casey pulled the pin on the grenade, counted to three and threw the small bomb so it would hit the side of the right wall and ricochet around the corner. What pool players would call a bank shot. The grenade exploded with a dull thump. There would be no more surprises, but now they'd have to move fast.

In his room Ho heard the cry of alarm and rolled out of his bunk. He still had his trousers on and didn't have time to put on anything else before the grenade exploded.

Troung also heard the cries and sounds of fighting. He yelled down the corridor from his room for men to come to him.

Casey was unable to get to Ho's room. Other Viets had gathered at the end of the corridor and he'd had to pull back to the barracks. From there shots flamed down the dim lit hallway till one hit the lamp and they were plunged into darkness.

Up on the surface, Phang's men felt the grenade explosion beneath them as only a small thump.

They got ready. In less than thirty seconds the first of the enemy below began to clamber out of the holes to reach the surface. As they stuck their heads up above ground, they were blinded by the force of the wind and beating rain that slammed against their eyes.

They were helped out by willing hands that tossed them one at time to their friends who swung eager blades. One by one, all that tried to reach the surface died, and not a shot had been fired. Forty-three VC lay with gaping wounds in their throats, draining their blood into the dark pools of water left by the storm.

Beneath them the rest of the VC were involved with trying to fight off the Kamserai. Troung had taken command of the situation.

He cried out down the hallway.

"Colonel Ho! Are you all right."

Ho stayed in the dark of his room, his pistol pointed at the entrance. Anyone who came in would die before they got him. At Troung's call he felt a surge of relief.

"Get me out of here!"

Troung tried. He forced his men to make an assault down the narrow passage, only to be met by grenades and automatic fire from the Kamserai. Eight men went down. Casey told Phang to give him his grenades. In the barracks he found an elbow's length of wood and tied the grenades to it in a bundle. He ran back to where he could get a clear throw down the hall, pulled the pin on one of the grenades and tossed the bundle. It hit the end of the hallway and fell to lie next to the body of the first Viet he'd killed. Troung and his men tried to scramble away. In the dark and the confusion they stumbled and bumped into each other. Several fell to be trampled on by their own comrades. The stick of grenades exploded, the force of the bombs rupturing ears and eyes. The ceiling groaned as the rafters holding up the surface weakened from the explosion and the rain. Timbers creaked as they shifted out of kilter.

Troung swore as he struggled to get out from under the pile of bodies that landed on him. Getting to his feet, he screamed for them to get some more men and some lights so they could see what they were shooting at. One of his men took him at his word, grabbed one of the oil lamps from its slot on the wall, lit the flame and threw the lamp down the hall to break and burn. The light of the oil was barely enough for Casey to get a look down the hall. He rose to his knees to make a try for Ho's room when a rapid burst of automatic fire nearly took his face off. He dropped back down.

In his room, Ho couldn't stand the tension anymore. He cried out to Troung to give him cover. From a musette bag he took out two grenades, pulled the pins, opened his door and threw them down the hallway toward the barracks. They didn't reach all the way landing twenty feet in front of the doorway. Casey, Phang and the Kams ducked for cover. The explosions of the grenades added to that of the previous ones and the smoke from the broken oil lamp made visibility in the corridor nil. Ho hit the door and scrambled as fast as he could on all fours to the safety of Troung and his men. Several shots, fired blind from the Kams, made him move faster than he'd have ever thought he was capable of.

Casey saw only the butt of Ho as he scrambled for cover. He rose to his feet and went after him. Shots from Troung made him take cover in Ho's vacant quarters.

Ho got to his feet aided by Troung, "What is going on? Who are they and how many of them are there? Where are our men?"

Troung had no answers for his master's questions. The roof of the tunnel began to sag as more beams were weakened. Water from the surface began to stream in through cracks. From the top, four of Phang's men dropped inside the tunnels. They wanted to reach their leader; instead they were met by Troung's people, each keeping the other pinned down. The ceiling creaked and shifted again as the walls of the tunnels started to buckle inward.

Phang yelled to Casey. "Get out of there. The whole damned place is starting to cave in!"

From the doorway, Casey knew that Phang was right. Clumps of sodden clay, mixed with palm thatch, were falling from the ceiling. He had to get out. The old fear of being buried alive forced him out of the room. Ho stuck his head around the corner to get a look at the attackers. He saw Casey standing in the light of the burning oil and smoke. Ho's face blanched at the sight of his nemesis.

He cried out "Devil!" and fired with his Tokarev. The 7.62 mm bullet hit Casey in the left shoulder, the copper-jacketed slug passing clean though him to bury itself in a timber. The force of the bullet spun him around. Casey turned back to see Ho taking aim again. He never had time. With no further warning, the roof of the tunnel suddenly dropped behind Casey then rolled over him

covering him up in tons of mud. Ho screamed
in glee. "We got him! The devil is done for
Troung!"

Phang could now see into the rain swept sky.
Waters from the surface poured in rivers into the
open cavity. He yelled for his men on the surface
to do it now! There was nothing he could do for
Casey. He was gone!

The Kams, fighting with Troung's men below,
backed up and climbed out of the tunnels. They
didn't want to be there in the next few minutes.

CHAPTER TWELVE

Phang's men cracked open the drums of gasoline and began pouring them down every hole they could find.

Smelling the gas fumes, Troung yelled at Ho. "They're going to try and burn us out!"

Ho grabbed Troung's arm and pulled him with him down a side corridor, where a sheet of tin lay flush against the wall between two upright beams.

"Help me!" he yelled, and grabbed the top of the tin sheet and pulled. Troung obeyed with eager hands. He thought he knew what his master had in mind. The tin sheet came loose. There was another tunnel concealed by the tin sheet that had been made for just such a purpose as this. Ho had kept it secret, even from his own men. One always needed a "hole card." He and Troung entered the dark tunnel and pulled the tin sheet back up behind them.

In the dark of the tunnels, men tried to find sanctuary. Smelling the gasoline fumes they knew what was going to happen. Several tried to rush out of the openings only to be cut down by rifle fire before their shoulders could get through the opening.

Phang was pulled out of the section of fallen tunnel by hanging on to a rifle butt. "Light the fires!'' he commanded as soon as he and the rest of his men were clear. White phosphorus grenades were tossed into the holes to lie on pools of gasoline, most of which had floated deep into the tunnels, riding on top of the flow of water from the rains.

Eye piercing brightness burst out of each hole as the white phosphorus grenades exploded. Almost simultaneously, the gasoline ignited. Black smoke billowed out of the holes as the fuel ate away the oxygen inside the tunnels, sucking the air out of the lungs of screaming men when they opened their mouths to cry for help.

Ho led Troung down a narrow passageway that led to the outside, clear of the village perimeters. Behind them, the sheet of tin served to keep the flames from coming after them. The cries of dying men being suffocated, or burned alive, sped their movements, till at last Ho moved away a covering of thatch and grass that let them escape to the outside world. The rain felt good, clean. Even the wind of the storm helped to clean the stench of burning human flesh from their nostrils and mouths.

A rolling ball of flame exploded, blasting off the door of the arms room, opening it up to the next wave of fire. The men outside felt a sudden draft of air going past them as the fire ate up what air remained in the tunnels and drew more to feed it from the outside. The influx of fresh air pushed another wall of flame into the arms room. Packed crates of 60 and 81 mm mortar rounds lay stacked by 122 mm rockets and open boxes of machine gun and rifle ammo. Hungrily, the flames attacked the wooden crates and washed around the heads of the rockets. The ammunition exploded. The surface ground erupted in several places. Gouts of smoke and flame burst through the surface of the earth to sizzle in midair as it came in contact with the rain. Clouds of steam rose to be washed away as the earth rippled and buckled. Phang and his men held onto whatever they could find to ride out this burning earthquake.

Several of the villagers' houses fell into the cracks that had opened up in the earth. Phang's men helped to pull the people out, carrying the injured to other houses to be cared for by their own. They had no time to give any more assistance. Things were still chaotic.

A group of eleven VC staggered out of the tunnel where the roof had fallen in on Casey. Dazed and in shock, they raised their eyes to the night and cried for help. Phang gave it to them. His men gathered around the pit. Instead of help, they gave them death as they fired round after round into the knot of men. Somehow others from the warrens below had found their way to the surface. Phang cursed. There must have been some exits his men had failed to cover. Those freeing themselves from the inferno beneath were in a state of shock, terror and confusion. Phang's men ran among them shooting them down or slicing them to ribbons with their machetes. Three ran for the wire to try and crawl out of their own camp. Bursts of automatic fire tore their backs and chests out of them leaving them hanging on the barbed wire.

From outside the camp, Ho and Troung watched for a few minutes as their men died. Silently they moved away and into the trees. They had to save themselves. That was their first duty. They were of vastly more importance than the few Bo Doi that were being slaughtered by the Kamserai barbarians. Ho would have Troung make a note to retaliate against the Kamserai by having ten of their people executed for each one of his that had died this night. That should please everyone. He had Troung lead the way. There might still be some of the animals in the trees.

Ho and Troung both felt that the night had not been a total loss. At least the one called Romain was finally done for. Ho knew his bullet had hit the bastard and now he was properly interred. Buried under a wall of mud!

Casca had covered up his head with his hand as the roof caved in on him. The weight of the mud pushed him down. He felt a heavy, crushing force come down on top of his body as a beam fell across him. He was pinned. The mud kept getting deeper over him. He tried to hold his breath, but it didn't make any difference. He couldn't breathe anyway. His nostrils and mouth filled with mud, choking off air that wasn't there. Trying to claw his way out, his right hand reached up toward the surface. Mud packed around it, keeping it in that position as blackness pulled him down. His last thought was of how long would he lie there.

The worst of the storm was passing. The winds had settled into a whine instead of a shriek. Phang and his men were soaked to the bone, their clothes sticking to them as though they'd been plastered to their skins.

The villagers stayed in their huts. Few even dared to look out their doors and when they did, they took only one quick look at the destruction and death about them and then quickly returned to the false security of their family units. They had seen that all of the Viets were dead, some lying around the camp face down in muddy water, but most would remain forever beneath their feet, in the graves they had dug for their own protection.

Phang's men wanted to leave. They could see no reason to stay any longer, and every minute they did added to the possibility of a relief force of VC coming. Phang shook his head. He looked down at the pit where Casca lay buried. It was his people's belief that one had to be buried in the graveyard where their fathers rested in order to find peace in the afterlife. He would do his friend this last service and see that he was returned to his own. It was a matter of honor.

He ordered his men into the pit. From the village a few shovels and picks had been found. His men worked in knee-deep mud, throwing the bodies of the dead Viets up to their friends. Then digging, shoveling and removing fallen beams, they searched through the mud. Rivers of rain running off the surface helped them as it flowed into the pit, washing away much of the mud and silt, flushing it down to the lower depths of the tunnels. A few bolts of lightning still split the night sky, providing brief periods of illumination for them to work by.

In one of those brief flashes of light, one of the Kams cried out. "I have found him!"

The rain had washed away a small channel along the length of a beam. Casey's right hand stuck up through the mud as if reaching for the heavens. Phang told them, "Be quick, but be careful. Don't use the picks if you don't have to."

They obeyed. Using their shovels and hands, they dug under the beam, freeing his body a bit at a time till they had his face clear enough to be washed clean of the mud by the sheets of rain. Tugging and pulling against the sucking mire, they finally had him free.

A stretcher had been prepared to carry him away. As he was laid in it, Phang looked at the still white face. With his own hand he cleaned it off as best he could, removing the clots of mud from his nose and mouth. It was said that it was through the mouth that the spirit left the body. He had seen many men die in his time, most of them from his own race, but this strange scarred, unhappy man somehow had touched him more than most.

Well, this was no time to dwell on it. He had many miles to go this night before they could rest. By dawn, with the passing of the storm, the VC would be after them. It would be best to be far away from this place. They would move back toward the South Vietnamese border. There, they would take Casey to the nearest American installation and turn his body over to them. Phang was sorry, not only for his friend, but that they had failed in their mission. Ho still lived, though many of his men had joined their ancestors. He did not know of what belief, if any, Casey had been, but once he was back in his home village he would make a sacrifice to his Gods for the Big Nose. It couldn't hurt.

Phang sent all of his men home with the booty from the camp, except for ten strong men to help him take Casey back. He hoped that if the Viets came after them they would try and follow the larger party. If they did that they would have little chance of catching them for here the Viets were in a foreign land and the Kamserai knew every inch of the terrain from here to the great salt marshes of the southern coast.

The makeshift stretcher was composed of a blanket between two poles. Phang covered Casey's face with part of it to keep the flies off. The ten men took turns at carrying their load, including Phang. The dark, silent little men had only one regret now that Casey was dead, and that was that they wished he didn't weigh so much.

The storm passed an hour before first light. The dawn would be bright and crystal clear. Much of the going was rough as they had to cross through areas where trees had been uprooted and every hollow and low in the ground was a swamp.

Crossing one of these small marshes, the stretcher slipped, spilling its load into the muddy fluid. Phang swore at the clumsiness of his men, even though he knew from experience the strain that carrying a dead man brought with it: the ache in the hands and shoulders, the hot burning ache that set right behind the neck and ran down between the shoulder blades.

He reached under the hip-deep water for the corpse, groping for a hand hold. He caught Casey by the collar and hauled him face up to the surface. Phang called for help and two of his men helped to drag and tug the body to dry land. Once they had it on land, they lay it down facing back the way it had come, the head lower than the body. One of Phang's men slipped and fell heavily across Casey's back. The weight of his body as he fell across Casey's rib cage expelled trapped air from the lungs.

Phang jumped as if he'd just been bitten by a snake. The air trapped inside of Casey came out of his lungs in a projectile burst. Plugs of brown mud and slime came with the air. The next most frightening thing was when the lungs sucked air back into them. Phang touched his good luck bag. Casey's body began to shiver and shake. His mouth opened and he vomited a fume of water and mucous from his stomach three feet straight into the air.

The Kamserai stood back in a mixture of wonder and superstitious fear as the dead man on the ground went into convulsions. Phang threw his body on top of Casey to hold him down as his heels drummed into the ground. He spasmed at the gut, jerking his body off the ground at the waist then slamming it back. Then he was still. His breathing had eased to a slight rattle, the legs still trembling a bit as his eyelids began to flicker.

Hoarsely, Casey managed to croak out the words, "Would you mind getting off of me? I got to take a leak."

Phang broke down in tears. Casey was not dead! He didn't know how or what had happened, but he knew that there were many things in this life that he had no explanations for. He had seen holy men who could be buried alive under sand for days and still live. To him this resurrection was no stranger a miracle than that. It was enough that Casey lived!

•   •   •

Ho was furious with the commander of the garrison in charge of security for the occupied region. The martinet would give him nothing in the way of men. The storm damage had been great and all of his men were needed for rescue and repair work. Also, if an attack were to come in strength, it would probably be at a time like this, when his lines of communication were in a severe state of disarray. Ho fumed and threatened to call Hanoi and General Giap. To this the commander only said:

"Of course, you may do that if you wish, Colonel. We still have shortwave radio communication with the north. By the way, if you do get General Giap on the line tell him his nephew wishes him well."

Ho left, knowing he had been outmaneuvered. But the game was not over. He and Troung would rebuild. Many of his agents had died in the tunnels, but there would be no shortage of volunteers to take their places. What he had to do now was return and recover what he could of his files and papers. The loss of those would mean weeks, if not months of reorganization.

CHAPTER THIRTEEN

He threw up a couple of times and went through a bout of the dry heaves before his stomach was able to hold any water. Every muscle in his body ached. Upon examination there were several large purple-black splotches along his rib cage and lower lumbar. The rest of him was just a mass of bruises of varying shades and hues. Trying to get to his feet was a major effort requiring the strong arms of Phang to assist him.

When he could finally speak coherently, his first question was: "Did we get him?"

Phang had to regretfully inform him that they had failed and apologized for the lack of success, taking all the blame on himself.

Casey leaned against a tree for support and shook his head to clear it of the remaining cobwebs.

"It's not your fault, Phang. Who could plan on the damned tunnel falling in. Besides which, maybe we did get lucky and the son of a bitch is buried back there in one of the tunnels or maybe the fires got him. If we didn't get him we'll know soon enough. If he's dead, it'll take some time before someone else will be able to take his place and get his teams reorganized and back into operation. If he's still alive then we can expect him to make it known by a wave of assassinations as soon as he can put the word out. He's going to be pissed as hell and that will be his way of letting us know about it.''

Phang agreed that Casey's analysis was probably correct.

''That is so, my friend. And we did have the pleasure of killing many of his men. The VC will not feel quite so secure in that area for some time to come. Now we have to get you back to your people. It is about ten more kilometers to the nearest South Vietnamese installation.''

Casey made part of the trip leaning on the arms of Phang's Kamserai. It took several clicks before his legs and body started to function properly again. By the time they reached the *Nhan Dan Tu ve* outpost where a People's Self-Defense Force guarded the approach to Tay Ninh he was moving if not with grace at least under his own power.

The sun was high in the clear sky when they reached the outpost. Phang had one of his men strip to the waist to show he was carrying no weapons and sent him up to the village gate. He and Casey waited out of rifle range until he returned with a squad of armed South Vietnamese under the command of an ARVIN officer.

Casey moved up to the front to greet them, knowing his Caucasian appearance might keep the South Viets from getting trigger happy at the sight of ten armed men carrying AKs and SKS rifles. The officer, a first lieutenant, had a good grasp of English and quickly understood that he was to radio Song Be and tell them that a Sgt. Romain was with them and to send a chopper to get him.

Casey took one of the Kam's AKs with him as well as a few magazines of ammo. Even if this was a People's Self-Defense Force village he wasn't going in unarmed. Phang was a bit reluctant to leave him until he knew that his friend was safely on his way to Song Be, but he also knew that the presence of his heavily armed Cambodians in the village would be unwelcome.

"I will leave you now. We have several days' march ahead of us before we reach our home grounds. Have your people contact me by radio to let me know that all is well with you."

All this he said in the presence of the Vietnamese officer.

"If I do not get word that all is well, then my men and I will know what to do and who to do it to."

He looked straight into the lieutenant's eyes when he said this. The warning, though veiled was clearly understood. The South Viet shivered as though someone had dug around his father's grave to make room for one more.

Casey shook his friend's hands. "You'll know and we'll meet again. Farewell, Old One, till then."

Phang waited till Casey had entered the gates of the village before turning his back to lead his men home. He had meant every word he had spoken. If harm came to his friend while in the village, he would return with all his warriors and put everyone and everything there to the sword. Not even the dogs or rats would be left alive to scratch among the ruins.

Gomez had been waiting at HQ since midnight. He knew there was nothing he could do, and until the storm passed he wouldn't be able to get a flight out to check over Ho's camp. But waiting by the radio was better than lying awake in his bunk all night listening to the howling of the winds outside and wondering what was happening. It was a strange feeling to be sitting with a hot cup of coffee in a warm building, while he knew that at that very moment men were fighting and dying in the dark. He felt strangely left out and somehow guilty for not being with them. He had requested that he be permitted to go along on the raid, but Tomlin had flatly refused and made it quite clear that if he did go, the best he could expect when he returned was a general court-martial and expulsion from the service. He was still there the next morning, red-eyed and suffering from a caffeine overdose when the storm passed and he was able to get a reconnaissance flight made over Ho's camp. When the report came in that the camp looked to be destroyed and there were many bodies in evidence all over the place, he called Tomlin to inform him that the camp had been hit though with what final results he didn't know. The colonel was relieved. It felt as though a rucksack full of sand had been taken from his shoulders. That ugly, scar-faced bastard had done it.

"Keep me informed when any more info comes in. I have to know if Ho was snuffed."

Gomez whispered under his breath. "I'm not sure that I wouldn't rather hear it was you."

It was nearly 1500 hours when he had the call come in from the PSDF village that Romain was with them. Rushing out of the office he told the radio man to call the chopper pad and have one waiting for him when he got there. He couldn't stay in the office any longer. He had to know what had gone down.

Gomez had the pilot land the Slick right in the center of the village blowing stray chickens into the air from the rotor blast. Casey was waiting for him. A South Viet officer gave him a hand getting into the bird, then turned his back to the whirl-wind as the chopper lifted off.

Gomez had the copilot radio HQ at Song Be that they were on their way back and Casey was all right. Yelling over the roar of the chopper, he asked, "How did it go? Are you okay?"

Casey shrugged his shoulders. "We don't know for certain if we got Ho or not, but we damned sure fucked up a lot of his people and his camp."

Gomez was almost pleased that Ho's death was not confirmed. That should give Tomlin a brand new set of nightmares for a while.

Song Be was not the only military installation to receive a radio message that hour.

The South Vietnamese officer made another call on his own radio. This time the message went to the Vietcong Command Center in the Parrot's Beak. He told them of the scar-faced American brought in by a party of Kamserai.

Colonel Ho van Tuyen was given a copy of the message. His face blanched as his lips drew tight and pale. He gave the message to Troung, who had much the same response.

"Comrade Troung, this has got to stop. Why is he still alive?" He stopped any response from Troung with an upraised hand in the form of a fist.

"We must have an end to him once and for all. I do not know what keeps him coming back to us but I do know that he will come again. *You!*" He pointed his shaking finger at Troung. "You must see that does not happen. You will go after him yourself. Kill him, once and for all, kill him. Bring me his head. I will have to look in the eyes myself before I can finally believe that he is truly dead."

He paused to try and regain control of himself. Sweat had broken out all over his body. His armpits stank with the superstitious fear of the unknown. "Go to Song Be! Go to Hong Kong. Go to the United States if you have to, but kill him." His voice rose to a near shriek. "Kill him, do you understand me. Kill him or I will kill you. Now go. Use any of our resources that you wish without restraint. But remember, my friend. Either he dies or you die. Now leave me."

Tomlin was not at all pleased with the after action report given him by Casey. The not knowing if Ho was dead was driving him nearly crazy. He had to admit that the operation had been successful in many aspects, but he didn't care if they had wiped out the entire Parrot's Beak. He wanted Ho dead so he could finally get a full night's sleep and not expect to wake up and find his throat slit from ear to ear.

Not knowing what else to do he dismissed Casey and Gomez.

"For God's sake go and clean yourself up. Every time you come in here you look like a garbage can. Gomez, can you do anything about this man's appearance?"

Gomez bit his tongue to hold back a response that would have sent him stateside in irons.

Tomlin redoubled his efforts to find out if Ho was still alive. Rewards of a thousand dollars in gold were now offered to any of his agents who could confirm Ho's status, dead or alive. He had to know. If Ho was still alive, then he would still need Sgt. Romain. He didn't like the man. He didn't like anyone that his rank couldn't intimidate, or who didn't defer to him with the respect he felt was his right. This, however, went beyond

his personal likes and dislikes. And Romain was
still the only one he knew of that had even come
close to killing that commie son of a bitch.

Casey was returned to the transient barracks
where Gomez left him alone. After a hot shower
and meal he hit the rack to sleep the clock around
twice. His body needed rest to heal fully. He slept
dreamless and deep the two days till a pounding in
his mind at last woke him. The pounding continued accompanied by a shout from Gomez.

"Get up damn you. You've got company here
and work to do."

Groaning, Casey crawled out of his bunk, put
on clean camouflage jungle fatigues to cover up
the scars on his body and unlocked the door.

Eyes still half stuck together with sleep, he tried
to focus on the face before him. The voice brought
recognition of his visitor before his eyes did.

"I say, you great bloody monster. Are you
going to sleep your bleeding life away? There's a
war to be fought and fair maids to rescue!"

His arms went around the slender almost girlish
frame of Van tran Tuyen. Van had long ago
learned to imitate cockney vernacular when he had
lived with his father in London. Casey wondered
if Van were related in some way to Ho but then
Tuyen was as common in Vietnam as Smith was in
the States.

Gomez grinned openly at the honest affection
being shown for each other by the two men. He
knew when to leave people alone. "Look you two.
Go and get some chow then come and see me at
HQ. I have some word concerning your little mission Romain. But it can wait an hour or two."

With Van at his side, Casey led the way to the
mess hall. Suddenly he was ravenous. While they

ate canned meat warmed into some kind of a stringy mush on top of powdered potatoes and a nondescript gravy of indeterminate origins, Van dropped his Limey accent.

"You don't look too good. But now that I'm here things will straighten out soon enough. I want you to fill me in on this thing with Colonel Ho. I just got in an hour ago and Captain Gomez said I should get it from you."

Casey stuffed his face with cook's gunk and swallowed. He felt much better now that Van was here. He'd first met the small handsome man a few months ago during an attack on a Special Forces camp in the delta. Since then a bond had developed between them that usually occurs only after one has known the other for years. Van was the only Vietnamese he completely trusted. Between bites of the gunk which Van passed on, he filled him in on what had been happening. He had the uneasy feeling that it wasn't over yet. If it had been, Gomez wouldn't have wanted them to come around after eating.

The day felt good. The sun was warm without burning into one's hide like a blow torch. He answered Van's questions as they crossed the compound to headquarters.

Gomez motioned for both of them to take seats and closed his office door. Resting a hip on the corner of his desk, he lowered his voice to make certain that no one other than these two men could hear what he was going to say.

"Ho is alive. He and his man Troung got out through an escape tunnel. One of our agents came to claim the reward that Tomlin put out. We even ran him through a sodium pentothal treatment to make sure he was telling the truth."

He waited a second to see if they had any questions. Neither one looked surprised to hear that Ho lived. Continuing, he moved back to his own chair and leaned over his desk. "Ho is sending the Bo Doi captain called Troung here to get you, Casey. From what our agent has told us, Ho has nearly as bad a case of the blind shits as does Tomlin. I don't know what you've done to the man but it has him on the edge of madness."

Casey volunteered nothing more and Gomez accepted it.

"This is the case. We will know when Troung comes into town. We've got one of his main agents spotted. When he makes contact we'll know about it. Then it'll be up to you guys to decide what to do. We still have to get Ho if any of us are ever to get any rest again. I'll run whatever interference I can for you with the Colonel but he's paranoid as hell. I don't think he really trusts me anymore because I don't have blue eyes. . . . Is there anything else you need to help with this thing?"

Casey looked at Van, thought a moment and said, "Yes. Bring me Phang. I think he deserves to be in on this operation all the way through."

Gomez nodded. "Okay, I'll get him here in the next couple of days because that's all the time you have before Troung arrives."

CHAPTER FOURTEEN

Dai Uy Troung came into town dressed in the guise of a field-worker. A conical hat of woven straw held to his head by a band of faded black cotton accented his standard peasant's dress of worn, threadbare black pajamas and rubber sandals. On his shoulders he carried a yoke, balancing two large earthenware jars containing smoked carp, ostensibly for the town markets. He came in the morning when traffic from the outlying towns was the heaviest and the road the most crowded. To his front and rear were others, also in peasant dress, who carried weapons and grenades beneath their jackets or in their baskets. If he was stopped they were to intercede, even if it meant having themselves arrested, or by creating enough confusion with their weapons that Troung could escape.

The security guards at the inspection posts never gave him more than a cursory glance. If they had, they might have noticed that his features did not have the worn-out, beaten look of reluctant acceptance of one's station in life that was characteristic of the peasants. That they didn't was just as well. One of the two security guards from the ARVIN on duty that day was a member of the local Vietcong Company and when he was not on duty for the Saigon forces he moonlighted for the Viets. If

Troung had given a certain phrase at the inspection station the VC sentry would have killed his companion.

A column of Armored Personnel Carriers passed him. They were filled with American soldiers heading for the field. He hated the sight of the pale, young, cocky faces, a cockiness that he knew would leave the first time they came under serious fire. These were not the real danger to his country. The young faces would go home or die here. The greatest danger, as always, came from the masses. Whoever controlled them controlled the country. And control came from more than money. A great portion of it came from fear and he had studied under a master. He would bring fear to this city and in so doing advance their cause.

That was ostensibly his purpose in coming to Song Be. Only he and Ho knew that what they really wanted was vengeance. Vengeance for the pain Troung had suffered and for the loss of face of his master. The attack on their camp was too great an insult to be tolerated. It should not have happened. Everything was the scar-faced sergeant's fault. He had given them more trouble than any of the American combat units or intelligence agencies. He had to be stopped. In the dark recesses of their minds both also knew they had to kill their own fear of the scar-faced man and the only way to end that fear was to face it. He would do that, but on his terms and with his weapons. When he had the American in his power then all the nightmares and pain he had suffered since that unspeakable offspring of a gutter dog had cut his hand off to get the briefcase would end.

Once inside the checkpoint Troung together with his escort moved by a circuitous route through the streets and narrow alleys to make certain they weren't being followed. At different points a member of his escort remained behind to stop anyone who might have been tailing them. Troung reached his destination, a bakery which supplied the local American garrison with bread and rolls for their tables. Across the alley from the bakery was a welding shop where plows and wrought iron fences were made or mended and sometimes weapons for the local guerrilla forces were repaired.

Colonel Tomlin called Casey and Gomez to him. There was a new secretary fresh from the States sitting at the desk. The Sp/4 had been reassigned to an Air Cavalry regiment and had been happily manning an M-60 light machine gun as a door gunner. Two days later he was in a body bag being sent back home. Heroes do not have much longevity.

Tomlin was agitated, his movements quick and jerky. His ashtray was full of half-smoked butts. He lit another one as he locked eyes with Casey and Gomez.

"He's here. The cock-sucker is here and I know he's coming after me!"

They knew who Tomlin meant. Gomez spoke for both of them. "Where is he? How many are with him?"

Tomlin put out his smoke. "He came in this morning. Right now Troung is at the bakery. One of the people there works for us. I just got the word ten minutes ago. Now I want you to take

care of him and find out where Ho is and come up
with some way to finish him off, once and for all.
And that's a goddamned order."

Both of them were pleased to hear the news and
so were Van and Phang who were back at the transient barracks waiting for them. They would have
to move fast. Since they'd made the hit on Ho's
headquarters another sixty South Vietnamese big
shots and eight Americans had been killed by Ho's
Ke' sat Nhan squads. Now that Troung himself
was on the scene the killings would probably
triple.

Gomez asked them if they wanted any help but
it was refused. Phang had brought a few of his
own men with him when he came in. This had
been their party from the beginning and they
would see it through to the end.

Troung questioned his agents about where the
one called Romain was. It was good to find out
that the Kamserai leader Phang was with him.
That way he could even all the scores at one time.
For now he was tired. It had been a long march
and he needed to rest. By tonight his men would
have the scarred one located, and he would see
that he was dead before the next nightfall, even if
it took the lives of every agent in Song Be. But for
now, he would rest a while in the bakery shop.

Phang moved through the alley with the totter-
ing steps of a man nearly blind drunk. His gray
hair and posture were that of an old man who only
found solace in his drink. The Vietcong in the
white shirt and slacks watching the alley saw nothing unusual about the old man. He was just

another example of the loss of dignity that had overtaken his people. He looked at the old man with disgust as Phang nearly lost his balance and went into a drunken sidestepping trot as if trying to catch his balance. He came close to the Vietnamese, his head hanging down, lips slack, eyes focussed on nothing.

Slurring his words, Phang mumbled as he nearly bumped into the guard, *"Toi hoan lai Ru cu Viang?"*

Raising his hand to push the drunk on his way, the guard told him, distaste dripping from his words at the sight of the old man, "I have no wine you old fool. Go away before you get hurt."

Phang bowed his head even further at the abuse, *"Xin Loi."*

He apologized then straightened up, his limp hand now filled with his knife. The blade sank up to the cross-guard in the Viet's throat. Phang leaned against him, pushing the man back against the wall holding him up as he forced the blade in deeper. Waving at Casey and Van he signaled with his arm for them to come over. Casey helped move the body out of sight behind the bamboo crates as Van stood watch.

Casey would have preferred not to have killed the guard but that was the only safe way they could get close enough to the building to get a look inside. If it was necessary they'd take the body with them when they left and just let Troung wonder what had happened to his man. It was always possible he'd think that he'd been picked up by a roving patrol.

Phang signaled for Casey to come closer. Pointing with the M-3 he showed Casey the window of the welding shop. From inside came a dim glow. He and Van moved silently to where they could get a look in the window. Behind them Phang and his Kamserai gave cover.

Troung stood with his back to the window talking to the welder-blacksmith. One other man stood with them, an American M-1 carbine held in his hands. Casey motioned for Van to come closer to the window. He could hear the people talking but couldn't understand all that was being said. Van leaned his dark head closer to the window and listened. Moving back from the window he whispered. "The one called Troung says that he is going to see that you and Phang are dead by tomorrow evening. Then he will get on with the rest of his mission. He plans on being in the city three days, then he will return to Colonel Ho in order to bring him up to date on the progress of their operations in this area."

Looking back at the window Casey sighed, "Well that's it then. We have to take him now before he gets away. If he gets out of the city and into the countryside we'll never be able to find him. Now, let's figure out how to do it."

Phang smiled, showing his betel nut stained teeth. "Just be patient, my friend. The one you want will have to come out sometime. There are only two exits and we will have both of them covered. When he does come out, we'll be waiting for him."

That plan made as much sense as anything else. If they broke in shooting, Troung might get killed before they had a chance to interrogate him. Troung would have to be taken alive and it would have to be done quietly. As for the others he didn't care, except that noise of gunfire might bring help to the enemy.

"All right, Phang, but it has to be quiet. When the door opens and Troung and his escort come out we'll take them, but I don't want anyone to start shooting. I'll take care of Troung myself. You and your men take out the one with the carbine and the blacksmith."

Phang bobbed his head in agreement, *"Xa Phai!"* He left Casey to give the orders to his men. Their firearms were put on their shoulders and knives brought out. One man went to the rear of the welding shop to cover the door there. It was not likely that Troung would use that door as he was known to be sleeping at the bakery across the alley.

Phang returned to the window to watch. Casey placed himself out of sight to the side of a door behind a stack of bamboo crates. Casey had Van change shirts with the dead Viet and take his place on guard. They were near the same size and, in the dark, from the back, Troung was not likely to notice the change until it was too late.

Phang watched Troung and the others inside. When he saw the Vietcong captain check his watch, he hissed at Casey, "Get ready, I think he's coming out!"

Nodding, Casey tried to make himself smaller in the shadows. Wearing the dead guard's shirt, Van moved so his face was better concealed from casual view.

The door to the shop opened. Troung was weary. It had been a long day and he had far to go tomorrow. He looked forward to his cot across the alley where the good smell of baking bread gave one comfortable dreams. His escort went out first, Troung followed close behind. The Bo Doi with the carbine talked to the back of the man with the white shirt he thought was his comrade. "Let's go."

He was sandwiched instantly between Phang and Van. Both had their knives moving at the same instant. Troung had no chance to make an outcry before his windpipe was squeezed shut by a strong hand and he was thrown to the ground. Inside the shop, the welder saw Troung go down in the open doorway and headed for the rear exit. His escape attempt was futile. Casey heard a muted cry from outside the rear door. Phang's other man came back in the door and held up his knife to show the blood on the blade.

Casey rose from Troung, looked at Phang and nodded with approval. "Nicely done, Old One. Now let's get the bodies back inside where we can have some privacy. There are a few things I have to ask this one when he comes to, which should be in just a couple of minutes." He pointed to Troung lying unconscious at his feet.

Van brought him some water from a bucket in the shop. A dousing combined with a few firm slaps across the face from Van's hand brought Troung back into the real world, a world which suddenly had become quite unpleasant.

Casey watched Troung's eyes as they frantically searched for any source of aid. There was none. In no face did he see any sign of compassion. Van's was especially discomforting. There was something very sinister about the look the handsome smooth-cheeked Vietnamese had in his eyes. Troung tried to move away and found he couldn't. His good hand had been chained to a steel ring welded on the anvil. The pulse in his temple pounded against the thin skin covering the bone. Casey said nothing; he had time. How much Troung could not have dreamed of. Van waited quietly by the brazier. Phang stood at his shoulder, his M-3 submachine gun held with the safety latch open, the bolt drawn back. He did not want his friends to be interrupted during this night's work. Outside on watch were two members of his tribe, both of them hard men who hated the communists for reasons of their own. They would stop anyone from becoming too inquisitive if Casey's questioning became a bit loud.

Troung suddenly saw everything in the welding shop in a new and sinister light. The only light came from the charcoal brazier. Its illumination did nothing to make things better, for it only gave off blood-red shadows that quivered and moved with the night. Van stood behind the brazier. At Casey's nod he removed from it a steel rod, the tip heated to white hot. He lit a cigarette with it then set the rod back in the brazier.

Casey spoke gently, almost regretfully.

"Captain Troung, I think it is time you answered a few questions for me. You know that you are already a dead man, but if you do as I say your death will be swift and painless."

Troung's throat was very dry and foul with the taste of fear in it. This was not supposed to be the way things were to have gone! And Americans were bound by the Geneva Convention. He found his voice.

"Sergeant, I demand that you turn me over to

the proper authorities!" His eyes pleaded with
those of the silent Van. "You are a South Vietnamese officer. Tell him that I am your prisoner."
If he could be given into the hands of the South
Vietnamese there was always a chance that his
escape could be arranged. Van spat a hunk of
phlegm into the red burning coals where it
popped, sizzled and disappeared in a tiny cloud of
steam.

Casey's face was that of a devil in the red glow
of the brazier. He shook his head as if talking to a
recalcitrant child, never raising his voice much
above that of a whisper.

"Captain Troung, I am the only authority you
will ever see. Don't think that you'll be turned
over to some weak-stomached American or to the
South Vietnamese, where you have agents. I am
the proper authority for you. I am your judge,
your jury, and I will be your executioner before
this night is done."

Troung's eyes jerked wildly in his head. The
bodies around him were mute testimony to the ac-
curacy of Casey's statement. He did not doubt for
one second that the scar-faced one meant every
word he spoke. He swallowed deeply and held his
breath as long as he could, then let it out. From
some unknown source he summoned up courage
he didn't know he had.

"I will tell you nothing."

Casey shook his head slowly back and forth.
"You are wrong. Very, very wrong. You will tell
me." His eyes touched those of Phang who
shrugged his shoulders. It meant nothing to him
what happened to the VC officer. He had seen

what the VC had done to his people and nothing the Big Nose and Van could do to this man could possibly be any worse.

Casey sighed deeply again, his words still filled with reluctant acceptance of what had to be done.

"I see that I am going to have to convince you." He stood up and moved, looking around the welding shop till he found what he wanted, a pair of metal shears. Standing behind Troung he raised his fist and struck him at the junction of his neck and shoulder hard enough to stun him without knocking him completely out. Before Troung's dulled mind could register what was happening, the heavy metal shears opened and closed. His little finger dropped to the dirty floor. Casey took the steel rod from the brazier and touched the tip of it to the knuckle stump, cauterizing the wound to stop the bleeding.

Troung started to scream at the searing pain of the red hot rod touching his raw flesh. The scream was muted when Casey slammed him again at the same junction between neck and shoulder. Troung whimpered in an agony of both body and mind. Never had he felt so helpless, emasculated and hopeless as he did now. For the first time he understood some of the terror that the captives he and Ho had taken had felt. He understood them much better, for now he was experiencing all that they had.

Casey leaned his face close to Troung's. "Now will you talk? Tell me the names of the rest of your agents here. And where I can find Ho?

Troung wanted to talk to stop the pain and fear, but somewhere he found the will to resist once more. He shook his head. "I will not talk."

Casey didn't like what he was doing and even had a kind of respect for Troung and his effort to hold out. But he would have what he wanted from him, even if it meant dismantling the captain one joint at a time.

Van moved closer to him. "I think it would be better if I took over. This is a thing that is best handled between us. I know his kind and what to do."

Van went to work after placing a block of wood between Troung's teeth to stop the worst of the screaming. Casey had never liked torture but what Troung knew could save the lives of many men. And what would be the worse crime, to go easy with the enemy and have dozens of his own die, or to do that which he felt he had to? If the VC had treated their own prisoners with honor, then he would have done the same. But it made no sense to let the enemy have all the cards and, when in Rome . . .

He told Van, "Get on with it."

Van knew from his own experience that at a certain point the body produced its own anesthetic and Troung would not feel most of the pain, except as a distant alien thing. He would detach his mind from what was being done to him. Van had no intention of letting it go that far.

Grabbing Troung by the hair, he pushed his face close to the brazier and held it there. Not close enough to set his hair on fire, but enough that the heat pounded at the flesh of his face, pushing through the surface skin deep into the meat. Red heat hammered at him. Troung could feel his eyebrows smoking, the flesh of his face starting to swell as the heat increased with every second. He would have screamed if the block of wood hadn't been jammed between his teeth. It was too much; he couldn't take this constantly increasing agony that he had no escape from. He broke, tears ran down his face, his body shuddered and trembled, and then went limp. He was not unconscious; he had just given up.

Van pulled Troung's blistered face back from the brazier and poured water on it from the tin bucket used to temper steel. He removed the wooden block and gave Troung some of the fluid to drink. He knew exactly what the Viet was feeling. He had seen many of the victims on whom the VC had used an identical treatment.

Softly, in Vietnamese, he asked Casey's questions again. "Tell my friend here who your agents are. Where can we find them and where is Colonel Ho? You might as well tell me now. You know that you're going to die anyway. You might as well save yourself some pain."

Troung didn't have it in him to even attempt a lie. He gave Casey the names of his agents in Song Be and told him that Ho was moving further south closer to the delta, but would be over the border in Cambodia near the town of Kampong.

Casey didn't recognize the name of the village that Troung had said was going to be used as a headquarters by Ho, but he knew Troung was telling the truth. Van looked at Casey and nodded to show that he agreed with him.

Casey moved closer to Troung who lay with his head on the anvil, sobbing.

"Good. If it makes you feel any better I'd like you to know that I have a great deal of respect for how much you have endured. But we both know that every man has a breaking point. It's just a matter of time till it's found. Now, you lived up to your end of the bargain and I'll live up to mine.''

Before the words could fully register, Casey's strong scarred hands grabbed Troung. Raising his head from the anvil, one hand on his chin the other at the back of his neck, Casey moved his hands in different directions. Troung's neck snapped and he went limp. Casey always tried to live up to his agreements. Troung had felt no pain and now his suffering was at an end.

Phang felt nothing for the dead Viet. To the contrary, he had a greater respect for his friend now that he knew that things were to be done in the Asian fashion. As for Van he had expected no less than what he had done. To both of them he spoke with quiet satisfaction:

''I know Kampong and the region around it quite well, my friends. If your Comrade Ho is there we'll find him. It is not far from my own territory. There aren't too many places there that would be suitable for a headquarters.''

Casey nodded his understanding. ''All right, Phang. We still have work to do tonight before the other assassins find out Troung is dead. We have to get as many of them as we can. Take me over to the Special Forces compound. I need to see a few people.''

CHAPTER FIFTEEN

They left the welding shop, leaving behind
Phang's Kamserai with orders to kill anyone who
came into the shop before dawn. The only visitors
the shop would have that night would have to be
Vietcong and therefore fair game. Casey, Phang
and Van returned to camp just long enough to
pick up Gomez and fill him in on what had taken
place. They also needed him to accompany them
to the Special Forces camp. He was well known
there. With him along they'd be heard a lot easier
and have a better chance of getting what they
needed from the Green Beret soldiers. Casey had
worked with them a time or two in the past and
liked their approach towards their work.

Gomez was excited about what they'd found
out and agreed that this was one time they had
better not rely on Tomlin to coordinate things.
There were still ten hours till dawn; much could be
done in that time if they moved fast. Before leaving Gomez made two calls. One was to his assis-
tant to whom he had given a copy of the list of
names Van had written down for him and then
told the man to run it through. He wanted
everything they had on the names within the hour.
Then he called over to the Special Forces C Team
HQ and told the Officer of the Day to get their

colonel up as well as their G2. He'd be there in twenty minutes.

The jeep ride over to the C Team was made through deserted streets and accompanied by the shriek of squealing tires. Gomez drove as though he thought he were in a Le Mans race. The jeep took corners dangerously. The narrow wheel base made it skip around every corner, threatening to turn over.

As they neared the Special Forces compound Gomez slowed the jeep down. He knew the sentries should be expecting him but it never hurt to play it safe. Those crazy men in the C Team had been known to shoot first and ask questions later.

The C Team compound was the best secured post in the province. The SFers didn't trust nobody. A searchlight hit the jeep as a strong voice with the definite texture of Birmingham Alabama to it, yelled out from behind a wall of sandbags and logs:

"Just take it easy there fellas and move up to the wire to where I can get a good look at you."

Gomez started to shift the jeep into low gear when the voice chastised him:

"Hey shit face, I said you, not the goddamned jeep. Now get a hustle on. I ain't got all night to stand here talking to a bunch of you no talent sons a bitches."

As the four men left the jeep the light went with them. When they were a few feet away from the gate the voice said, "That's jest about far enough. Now here's what you do. I want the Viet and . . ." The voice paused for a second as the light moved on to Phang's face. "I want the Viet and the old Kamserai to move up first, just to make sure that you Yankees don't have a gun in your back.''

Gomez started to protest. "Now you listen to me, whoever you are. I am a captain in the United States Army and I'm telling you to stop this bullshit and let us in. And that's an order!"

The voice laughed as the sound of a rifle bolt loading a round in the chamber floated over to them.

"Well then, Captain, let me clear up this here misunderstanding. I don't give a shit if you're Andy Jackson. This is our homestead and we make the rules and as far as your order goes, what are you going to do, send me to Vietnam? Shit it's my third tour now. You got ten seconds to do as I said or I'm going to kill them two Oriental gentlemen right where they stand and then I'm going to think real hard about you two for another three seconds. Now come on or get out!"

Gomez didn't know what to say or do but Van just grinned and moved closer to the wire, his hands up where they could be clearly seen. Phang went with him. A Chinese Nung mercenary from Cholon moved out to the wire through a narrow passage. He looked them over, made them hand over their weapons then took them inside. A minute later the voice called back. "Okay, fellers, you come on in now, hear?"

Gomez was still fuming as they were admitted to the compound. Once the searchlight was out of their eyes and Gomez could see again he focused on the source of the southern drawl. SFC Jim Gilbride had an angular face with a gap between his front teeth, set on top of a body standing six foot three. The tiger-striped camouflage fatigues and matching soft cap did nothing to make Gomez think the bastard would have not been better off behind a brace of mules in someone's south forty.

"Nothing personal now fellers, just making sure. You come on with me. Our boss is waiting for you and it better be important. He don't like losing sleep over bullshit."

Gomez could think of nothing to respond with. It was quite obvious the man didn't care what Gomez said or threatened him with. Casey just grinned. He knew the SFC's type and he was the kind that he'd want behind or in front of him if the shit got heavy. He was a stayer and a doer.

As they went across the outer compound Casey saw the defenses were in echelon. Between the main gate and the inner compound was a wall of sandbags with firing pits set in them at regular intervals and a string of claymores facing out going around the entire inner perimeter. Security was handled mostly by Nungs from the Chinese colony in Cholon. They were good, tough fighters who hated the communists—though they did have a tendency to cheat at cards and dice and therefore didn't get along very well with some of the Montagnard tribesmen who took a dim view of such practices.

One thing he knew about this camp, there would be no one asleep on guard. Roving patrols of Nung noncoms and Special Forces men could be seen going on their rounds checking every bunker and man.

Gilbride escorted them to the C Team's headquarters where he politely opened the door for them and showed them in. Lt. Colonel Mitch Wardell was waiting for them, sitting at a table normally used for poker and sipping on a cup of coffee. He was fully dressed in the same tiger-striped fatigues as was Gilbride, a forty-five resting on his hip and an M-16 leaning up against the corner of the table.

Lt. Colonel Wardell had a square jaw set under a fighter's bent nose. "You guys want coffee or do we just get on to why you pulled me out of the rack instead of going to your people at MACV?"

Gomez cleared his throat. This man was much more fightening than his own colonel even though he wasn't in his command. "No coffee, sir, and after I explain things I think you'll see the reason why we're here rather than MACV."

Wardell indicated for all of them to take seats. As they did he gave a curious look to Van in his white shirt and Phang, who studiously ignored the colonel's examination. Casey thought Phang and Gilbride would probably get along very well together. Neither one really gave a crap about authority.

Casey helped himself to a cup of coffee as Gomez explained what was coming down and why they were there. It didn't take Wardell two minutes to analyze the situation and come to a decision.

"You came to the right place. My G2 is next door. Give me a copy of your list of names and I'll get him on it through our files. We got friends with Delta project and Sergeant of the Guard that may be able to help us." He took the list, checked over the twenty-four names on it and whistled between his teeth. "I know some of these bastards. Two of them work for us as interpreters and there're a couple of others that are civilian administrators. The shit's going to hit the fan tonight." He tossed the list to Gilbride.

"Gilbride, get your rebel ass in gear. We're going possum hunting tonight. Tell Captain

Hardy to run these through and do it ASAP. While he's doing that I want you to get the boys ready to move. Split the team in two and leave behind those who were on the last operation to take care of the fort. Have the rest take full kit and weapons. Get me enough vehicles from the motor pool to make up six teams. Also tell the commander of the Nungs to break loose B company for me. We'll spread them out among us for a little extra muscle. Now get going you ill educated, insubordinate, red-neck bastard."

Gilbride grinned, showing the gap between his teeth. He threw Wardell a sloppy half salute and took off on the double. The only thing he liked better than pissing the brass off was a good fight.

Captain Hardy came in with his report while the C Team was getting ready and vehicles and ammo distributed among the raiding party. The Nungs were especially pleased at the prospect of action though they didn't know yet that they were going to be fighting in town. To them it didn't make any difference. Wherever the Special Forces men said they go, they went, and did what was expected of them.

Hardy handed over his list to Wardell. "Sir, we have a fix on sixteen of the names that are in town. There are three more in the outlying villages and two who are members of the ARVIN company attached to MACV."

Wardell adjusted the straps on his shoulder harness and grunted. "That's better than I expected." To Gomez he snapped, "You think there's any sense in taking prisoners? If I'm not mistaken this damned thing is probably set up in cells where no one knows who the others are."

Gomez looked at Casey before answering. "I

wouldn't go through any great deal of trouble to take any alive. If it's possible to do it without any of your people getting hurt then there might be a bonus there somewhere."

Wardell sucked in his gut, psyching himself up for the job. "That's the way it goes down then. Not having to take 'em alive makes things a lot easier."

In the compound the Nungs were in ranks ready to load. The Special Forces men stood with them. No trace of sleep in their eyes, they had the look of hunters who were just a bit hungry.

Wardell climbed in the shotgun seat of a weapons carrier as he gave his orders to his men. He divided them up into flying teams, each with a list of names and addresses supplied by Captain Hardy who was thoroughly pissed that he was to be left behind.

Before he moved out Wardell thought of something and called Gomez back over to him. "Want to do me a favor son? Those two agents in the ARVIN are assigned to the detachment at your camp. What say you run over there and snuff them for us. It'd be a lot easier then me sending some of my men roaring up there like a bunch of outlaws. This way your boss can get some credit too and not feel left out."

Gomez was pleased that he was finally going to get to do something positive. "It will be a pleasure, sir."

Wardell grunted an acknowledgment, raised his hands in a circling motion over his head and pointed to the gate. "Open that son of a bitch up and lets get to it!"

The small convoy moved out. As soon as they hit the first intersection jeeps and trucks began to split up heading for their target areas.

Hardy cursed after them and went back to the HQ. He had to make a couple of calls before the shit hit the fan. He had to let the South Viet-namese police and military know that it was going to get noisy in town tonight and it would be best if they stayed in their barracks and guard posts. Anyone on the streets of Song Be tonight would be considered fair game.

At first Gomez had felt a bit insulted that War-dell hadn't even asked them if they wanted to go along for the ride. It didn't bother Casey or Van. They knew the Special Forces men would do the job right and didn't need their help now that they had the names and numbers. Casey knew what was bugging Gomez. The captain felt that he was superfluous and hadn't contributed his fair share to their mission. Casey whispered to Van and Phang who nodded their heads in agreement and then nudged Gomez. "Captain, what the hell are we standing around here for. There're two agents right in your own back yard waiting for you. And they're all yours. We'll just lay back while you do the deed."

Gomez yelped out, "Then let's get to it. But how are we going to get the ARVINs to tell us where they're located?"

Casey climbed in the shotgun seat of the jeep as Gomez kicked over the motor. "We'll figure that out on the way."

CHAPTER SIXTEEN

On the way back to MACV, Phang asked about his men at the welding shop.

"Let's just leave them there for now. I don't want Troung's body moved. I think we may have a use for it later."

When they were checked and readmitted to the MACV compound Gomez asked him, "Well, have you come up with a way to get them?"

Casey smiled. "Let's use the system. You call the ARVIN Commander and tell him there is an operation coming down and you want a couple of his people to assist us in planning. Just give him their names and say that you need them because of where they are from. That should be enough."

Gomez nodded; that was simple enough. If the agents were told they were needed to help in an operation, they would probably double-time over to his office to find out what it was about.

He pulled into his parking spot and led the way inside. The OD was a lieutenant who had been in the country only a couple of weeks.

"Lt. Jansen. Get the ARVIN commander on the line for me. Once you've done that you are relieved of duty and are to return to your quarters. I'll take over for you here."

Jansen did as he was ordered though he wondered why Gomez had such a disreputable looking group with him. After making the call and patching it through to Gomez's office he exited the scene with a feeling that he was doing the right thing. There was an aura about those men that he didn't like and he was glad that Gomez had told him to get his ass out of the way.

After he put the phone back on its receiver his hands were shaking a bit.

"The ARVIN Commander said he'll have them sent right over. I promised to fill him in on the details of the new operation in the morning, that right now we were just in a state of preplanning."

Gomez was becoming a bit more nervous. His hands began to sweat as they waited. He checked his pistol making certain the safety was off and there was a round in the chamber. He did this three times before Casey told him, "Just relax, Captain. This is your chance to question them. When they come in just lay your piece on them. Phang and I will shake them down and then, they're all yours. Just don't get excited. I know this is different from being in the field but it'll work out all right."

Neither of the two ARVIN soldiers knew that the other one was also a member of the *Ke' sat Nhan*. All they knew was that one *Ngu Huang* had been pulled off of guard duty and the other *Bo Chui Than* was taken from his bunk and both ordered to report to the American Headquarters at MACV. They would have been a bit suspicious if they had been searched, forced to give up their weapons and delivered with an escort. As this did not occur and they had been told they were wanted only because of where they came from, and that the Americans only wished some information about their home villages, they had no inkling of what was about to take place.

Casey was waiting in the outer offices when they made their appearance. He was casual as he indicated they were to leave their arms in a rack set there for that purpose. They did and were hustled into Gomez's office where they reported.

It was the sight of Phang combined with Casey that brought a rush of memory to Bo Than. He had been briefed earlier on his targets and his alternates. One of his targets was an American sergeant with a scar on his face. He had also been told of the attack on their base camp by the Kamserai tribesmen. From the looks on everyone's faces he knew something was definitely wrong. Without hesitation he drew his bayonet and lunged at the Sergeant. Casey had moved to block the thrust of the blade, when a sudden ear deafening double blast blew Bo Than sideways across the room. Both of the heavy grained slugs from Gomez's forty-five auto had hit the Viet in the rib cage, blasting holes in him large enough to stick a grown man's fist through.

Things had happened too fast for Ngu to make any response. When Bo Than had moved so did Phang who now had his own knife pointed under Ngu's left ear. Van searched him while Casey checked over the other one's body. Neither one had anything on them that could be of use. No papers, no other weapons.

Ngu was placed in one of the metal backed gray chairs and tied down with some riser cord found in one of the desks in the outer offices.

Ngu understood quite clearly his options. He was to tell all that he knew which wasn't very much. He had only the two names of the men that were in his cell. He also knew that he was a dead man even if he did talk. He would never be made into a Kit Carson, one of those former VC who had turned coats and chosen to work for the Americans in exchange for amnesty and money.

Gomez was just getting settled back to begin his interrogation when Ngu made his decision. None of the men in the room had any idea what he was doing till they saw his face start to turn black and his eyes roll up in the back of his head.

Casey grabbed him by the face and forced his mouth open. A gout of bright red blood gushed forth spewing across the room and covering Casey's hands.

"Goddamn it! The son of a bitch has bitten his tongue off and swallowed it!"

He tried to force his fingers in far enough to remove the hunk of severed tongue but it was too slippery from the blood for him to get a grip on it.

Ngu went into spasms. His bladder and bowels released themselves. Casey took Phang's knife from him to try and open an airway in his esophagus but it was too late. Ngu shivered then quit moving. Casey didn't know if he had died of suffocation or had drowned in his own blood. It didn't make any difference. The man was dead and would tell them nothing. Still the night hadn't been a complete loss. They had taken out two of Comrade Ho's assassins and knew that right now Wardell and his men were out removing more of them from this vale of tears.

It was a miniature 'Night of the Long Knives.' All through the city doors were kicked open and men hauled from their beds to be shot or bayoneted. Radio communication kept Wardell informed of the progress of his operation. There had been a couple of *Ke' sat Nhan* who had man-

aged to get hold of weapons before being taken
out. Two of his SFers had been hit but it was
nothing serious and three Nungs got nailed, two of
whom had died. Of those who had been able to get
their hands on weapons and resist, three had com-
mitted suicide when they realized there was no
escape.

The South Vietnamese police and military did
as they had been requested. They stayed at their
posts and brought in any roving patrols. The
sounds of gunfire throughout the city lasted till
nearly dawn when peace came with the rising sun.

While they waited, Casey and his men went over
the maps of the region around Kompot. Phang
pointed out the exact location of his village. Oddly
enough, it was less than five kilometers from Ho.
Casey pointed to a spot on the map and asked
Phang about it. The Kamserai chieftain had nothing good to say about the place. Casey recalled a
similar place in World War Two into which the
British had forced a Japanese unit to enter. It
sounded like just what he needed. They went over
the plan until the phone rang.

It was a tired, but satisfied lieutenant colonel
that called Gomez on the phone from the C Team
HQ.

"Captain Gomez, this is Wardell. Just wanted
to call and fill you in. We got all of them but two,
who weren't where they were supposed to be, but
we have a lead on them and will get them later.
How did you do?" He paused, then grinned into
the receiver of the phone. "Well then, that's good.
Bit his own tongue off eh? Sounds like someone
I'd like to have on my side. Anything else me and
my boys can do for you? We owe you one and like
to pay our debts."

There was muted conference on Gomez's side of the phone before Wardell cleared his throat and spoke again. "All right! If that's what you want then that's what you'll get. Have your people at our chopper pad at 0700 hours and we'll get on with it."

Gomez leaned back in his chair; he felt good. At last he had tasted a bit of action and didn't feel so left out anymore. "Colonel Wardell says it's a go and for you to be at his chopper pad at 0700 hours. He looked at his watch. You've got less than an hour so take my jeep—and good hunting. I'll take care of Tomlin. All I have to do is say that these two were the ones assigned to kill him and he won't worry about anything else." Gomez looked at the faces of the three men and shook his head. "Gods, this is madness. But this is one time I won't feel bad about being left behind. I don't think you have a snowball's chance in hell of pulling it off, but then you're the experts. Good luck!"

They made a quick detour back to the welding shop before heading over to the SF compound. They took with them Phang's Kamserai and an oddly bulging duffle bag.

Wardell was waiting for them when they arrived. He knew from the shape of it what was in the bag but didn't ask what it was for. There were some things it was better not to question. The Huey was already throbbing and vibrating as if eager to get in the air and deliver its cargo and get back to a more understandable kind of war.

The chopper took off with its odd cargo heading east and then south across the border back to Cambodia. The pilot looked with distaste at the duffle bag, but like Wardell thought it best not to ask any questions. What you didn't know, you couldn't talk about, and he was sure this was one flight he would probably want to forget as soon as possible.

First they went to the spot on the map that Phang had told Casey of. The pilot set down in a clearing and kept the motor idling as Casey and Van moved out to get a look at the terrain. Phang wouldn't go in. He and his men set up lookouts till Casey and Van returned. It took them about an hour before they came back, muddy and tired. Casey nodded his head in agreement. "You weren't bullshitting Phang. We saw them and they're everything you said they were."

Van merely had a look of awe on his face as he tried to imagine the consequences of his friend's proposed action. It was terrifying.

Casey had the pilot fly them around checking reference points on his maps as Phang pointed out landmarks. At last Casey told him to take the Kamserai chieftain and his men home.

Phang unloaded leaving the duffle bag behind. Casey wasn't through with it yet. Casey made the pilot wait on the deck a few more minutes until Phang returned and handed him two leather water bags connected at the spouts to each other by a broad strap, which Casey hung around his neck.

"I will be waiting by the clearing I showed you. Good hunting my friends."

The pilot was getting the jitters. He felt a great sense of relief when Casey told him:

"Just one more little flyover and then you can set us down where we get off and you can go home."

The pilot bobbed his head in agreement.

"That sounds good to me. I don't know and

don't want to know what the hell you people are up to but I don't like it. I'm just a taxi driver and that's all I want to be. The sooner you get out of this machine the better I'll feel."

Casey gave him his heading and they headed off over the tree tops at about five thousand feet. The flight took less than fifteen minutes before Van pointed out his side of the chopper and yelled:

"I think that's it!"

Casey leaned out to get a look. Van was right. Ho's new base camp was coming up fast. He told the pilot to circle it staying high. Even from their altitude he could see a thatch-roofed building where a VC flag flew from a bamboo pole. That had to be it. Casey noticed that Comrade Ho had changed his living style. He didn't seem to like being underground anymore. Casey opened the duffle bag, took out his bayonet, reached inside the bag with it and began to cut.

Colonel Ho heard the chopper and rushed out of his thatch roofed building to get a look. It was flying high. He told his men not to fire. There was something strange about it. The chopper was not making an assault pass; it was just doing a long lazy orbit. What was *that*? Ho shaded his eyes to see better. The chopper was right over him and something was falling from it. Something small. Was it some kind of new bomb? With a cry of alarm he threw his body into a nearby slit trench and covered up his head. He heard a dull thump as the object hit the ground. Nothing more happened. Cautiously he raised his head to get a look.

The object was less than five feet away from his face. His bowels turned to ice water. It was a human hand. He knew who it had belonged to and who it had to be in the helicopter that dropped it.

That madman with the scarred face was still with him. Troung had failed in his mission and now the thing was here to haunt him, flying over him like a bad spirit. If he would come down to the earth and fight, then he, Colonel Ho van Tuyen, would end it right now. What was this? The chopper was coming down lower, heading for a clearing a few hundred meters to the south of his camp. Would the madman dare . . . ?

Ho ran to the south calling his men to come with him.

They had just reached the edge of the clearing when they saw Casey standing alone in the field, a bag at his feet. Curiously, the helicopter had taken off and left the American there alone. Why?

To Ho it made no difference anymore. He could see the object of his hate standing there, mocking him. With a cry he ordered his men, all good soldiers from the crack 213th PAVN, to get him. As they rushed across the field, Casey turned and ran toward the south.

When the chopper had set it down it had first made a low pass near a line of trees at the far side of the clearing and Van had jumped out. He was now watching Ho as he went after Casey. To him it was like sending a pack of rabbits to chase a tiger. He almost felt sorry for the rabbits.

CHAPTER SEVENTEEN

Ho stopped at the duffle bag. He knew what was inside of it. Still, he had to see it. He ordered one of his men to take out the body. It was one thing to see a detached hand lying in the dust, but to see his former aide lying there with both of them removed at the wrist, the face blistered and distorted, made him cry out in rage and frustration, the likes of which Ho had never known before.

"I will have him." To his men he said, "Bring two companies from the camp. Take nothing but weapons. I will follow that dog into the bowels of hell itself, but I must have him!"

Ho's men looked at him with confusion and fear on their faces. What was this devil riding him? There had been stories told by those that had served him before of his vendetta against one American sergeant. The man who brought the bag with the body of Captain Troung; it must be him.

Ho's company commanders did not mind too much that he was ordering two hundred and forty men to chase after one. In the last few weeks there had been little action for them because they had been refitting and retraining. This would provide a pleasant break in their routine. A hunt was always welcome and it would do their new men good to get out and taste blood. Yes, the chase could be very good for morale.

The first indication that it might not be as easy as it looked was when a Bo Doi's face exploded. The American had not run very far. . . .

Casey lowered his weapon from his shoulder, the familiar, thin wisp of blue tinged vapor trickling out the bore of the M-3. That should get them moving. The leather bottles around his neck gurgled thickly as he moved.

He took off again before the first return fire came his way. Dodging and weaving through the low brush and trees, he kept moving south. Behind him he could hear the enemy calling to each other as they spread out. They were not coming as fast as they could have. Getting one of their own killed right off slowed their feet a bit.

He ran till he was far enough ahead of them to take the time to prepare for them a small present. Then he moved on again careful to leave a trail that a blind man could see.

Van stayed with the 213th keeping behind them and out of sight. He had to time things right. He was a hundred meters to their rear when he heard a cry of pain.

Ho was behind the point man lashing him with his tongue to hurry up when the man suddenly bent over at the waist. Red, bloody stakes stuck out of his back. He was impaled on a Malay gate, a strong, bent sapling with sharpened stakes tied to it. When the release cord was hit, it would swing out and slap the unwary victim right in the belly. It was a favorite trick of the VC.

He called his company commanders over to

him. "No more stalling. He is close. Even I can see his trail. I know that he is leaving it for us to follow and we will, because he is at the end of it and he is not moving back to the Vietnamese border. He is heading due south. Soon he will reach the sea and there will be nowhere else for him to go. He will have to make a stand. Then we will take him. By all the gods of my fathers we *will* take him."

The sun passed its high mark and the shadows began to grow longer and still the chase continued. Three more men fell to bullets from Casey's sub-machine gun. Another Viet who thought he had him spotted, and in his eagerness had run to the forefront wanting to be in at the kill, was found by his comrades, hanging by his feet from the branches of a tree, his throat slit from ear to ear. He was left to drain like a slaughtered hog.

The new men of the 213th didn't like this chase. It was not going as they had expected. They were the ones doing the dying. Ho noticed the reluctance on the part of several of them to speed up their steps. This was corrected with two quick pistol shots to the brains of the nearest slackers. His message was clear. Go after the American and maybe die, or slow your steps and die for certain. The choice was clear; the pace picked up.

Phang waited with his men at the clearing he had shown Casey from the chopper. He didn't know if their plan was working or not, but he had faith in his big-nosed friend's ability to do the extraordinary. Van would come soon. The sun was nearly at the level of the tallest trees. He would have to come soon.

When Ho and the 213th reached a small shallow

stream Van knew it was time for him to leave. They were on the right track and the timing was good. He cut off to the west leaving the rabbits to try and catch their tiger.

Casey had stopped only long enough to wash his face in the stream. His fatigues stuck to him like glue but he knew the Viets were in the same shape. He wanted them tired for the time when they would make mistakes. He checked the sun and his watch; he'd have to hurry. Both on and off the trail he set up trip wires, some attached to grenades, others to nothing. When the first Bo Doi hit a trip wire his right leg was blown off at the knee and shrapnel sliced open the arm of the man behind him, who was glad of the wound, for now he could stop the chase and go back to camp. He was left where he was to rest and make it back under his own power. Ho would spare no able-bodied man from the pursuit.

The next time one of the Viets hit a trip wire he screamed and hit the deck as did all those around him. Nothing happened. Afraid to move and afraid to stay in place they didn't do anything till Ho pulled his pistol from his holster. They rose and examined the wire finding it led to nothing. Ho was furious.

"The beast mocks us. He toys with us as if we were mindless children. Up! Up! and after him!" They ran till they hit another wire which didn't kill but knocked out of commission two more men of the valiant 213th.

Once they were across another clearing Ho spotted Casey, who waved for him to come on. Ho did. His mind slipped into a singleness of purpose that would allow nothing else to enter. He drove his men as he drove himself after the *Qui than;* he had to be a demon to torment him so.

Ho and his men continued their hot pursuit, but the men for other reasons. They were more terrified of the madness they saw in Ho's eyes than they were of the lone American. The yankee might be able to kill a few of them but Ho could have all of their heads. Their odds of staying alive were still better if they chased the American. And perhaps he would kill Comrade Ho. . . .

Van neared the clearing. His coming had been announced by Phang's scouts who had been set on the trail with orders to tell him as soon as they saw Van approach. His men were on their feet and ready. Breathless, Van gasped out, "It is time. They are nearly there. If we go now we'll just make it."

Van was tired but refused the offer to rest and follow later. Phang admired the young Vietnamese. He was the only one of that race he had ever liked. In a spontaneous demonstration of his feelings he called over one of his men who carried a canvas rifle bag. From it he removed one of his most prized possessions, a cut down twelve gauge Savage automatic shotgun and a sack of ammo for it. He placed the weapon in Van's hands saying, "Take this. It will serve you well this night. It is yours to keep."

Van was moved at both the gift and gesture. He bowed his head in respect before Phang, who gently raised him to his feet. "Now, my son, we have work to do."

Phang took the lead. He knew the paths of this land as he did those of his village. There would be no slow feet with his men. They nearly ran, also

heading to the south. Van caught his second wind
and kept up with them, though at times he thought
his heart was going to leap out of his thin chest.

Casey could smell it now. He hunched down by
a fallen log and waited. He was a few minutes in
front of the PAVN and the respite was welcome. It
gave his body time to regulate itself, the heart to
slow its heavy pumping, the tremor in the legs and
arms to ease. He waited.

He could hear them coming through the brush.
He put a fresh magazine in the smg, placed his last
two grenades beside him and took a careful look
over the top of the log. The first Viets were entering the clearing. In spite of Ho's urgings they
moved a bit slower than normal. Ho could not
take the time out to set another example. He felt
they would have his men cornered any time now.

Five, then ten, then twenty of them came out of
the trees in a skirmish line. Casey pulled the pins
from the grenades, took a breath, released the
hammers counted to three and heaved them, one
after the other over the log, not looking to see
where they landed. Two dull thumps accented by
screams for *Bac si,* medics, broke the silence. He
rolled up to the top of the log, set his weapon on
it and began to hose down the PAVN troops.
Rounds came back at him instantly, eating chunks
out of the log and peppering his face with wood
splinters. They were getting a little bit pissed, he
thought, as he rolled out of sight eventually rising
to his knees. He ignored the whistling of bullets
overhead. Twice a couple of rounds came close
enough to his ear so that they sounded like someone clapping his hands together.

From this point on he watched for the landmarks that they had made earlier. He found a giant Mango tree with a ripped trunk by a small pond. He knew exactly where he was and where he was going.

The sun was nearly down and death silently waited in the coming dark. He ran at full speed now. There was no way for Ho to miss his route. They would come.

Phang cocked his head to the side and nudged Van who had come up alongside of him. "Gunfire, I hear gunfire not far away." Van tried to listen, but all he heard were the sounds of the night wind and the leaves rustling in the trees. Phang grinned; his senses were more acute than those of one raised in the city. "Trust me young Van. There is gunfire and that means that Casey is still going. He should almost be there by now. Come we must hurry!"

CHAPTER EIGHTEEN

The salt marsh waited in the moonlight, its waters black enough to suck the soul from anyone unwary enough to set foot in it. Bubbles of marsh gas broke through to the surface adding the pungent odor of decayed vegetation to the smell of stagnant water. Patches of reeds grew in clusters, hanging together as if they needed each other for support. Darker shadows rose above the still waters, arms stretched out, moss hanging from their limbs beckoning, waving to and fro in the night breeze coming from the land. Huge mangrove trees stood on raised crablike roots. From a distance they appeared to be huge contorted bodies that only needed the breath of life to be able to rise on their roots and walk.

Casey began to wade into the murky waters. Stripping his camouflage jacket from his body, he let it fall to float on the surface like a patch of mottled moss. From around his neck hung two large goatskin bags. On his shoulder, a strap held his grease gun in place. Extra magazines were in his hip pack. He had all that he needed with him. This was the place. Here he would wait for Ho to come to him. From behind him he could hear the PAVN soldiers searching for him. His mind cast back to another time in the past when he had been

with the Legion and had used swamps similar to
this. That time it had been only to escape his pur-
suers; this time it was to trap them.

From the distance came a cry with a note of
discovery in it. He knew that his trail had been
found. Soon they would be at the spot where he
had let his jacket fall. They knew that he was
alone and would feel confident. This didn't bother
him. The dark waters and black night would more
than make up for the loss of any allies. No! They
were his allies, his army. He would not be alone
this night; others would come to his aid.

Let Ho and his men come into the waters where
he'd be waiting to take them. Once they were com-
mitted, Van and Phang would do as they'd been
told; and between Casey, the marsh, Van, and
Phang's Kamserai there would be a great killing
this night in the hours before dawn. Bending over,
he lowered his hands into the calf-high waters,
sunk them deep and pulled up a double handful of
thick syrupy bottom mud. He smeared it all over
his body and face so that even from a distance of
three feet he would be hard to see. He went deeper
into the swamp, the mud sucking at his feet,
threatening to pull his jungle boots off. Well,
if the swamp wanted them then let it have them.
Untying the laces he let the boots sink. It would be
easier for him to move without them.

The water was shallow now but when the tide
came in it would raise the level to above his waist.
Casey knew that something else would also come
in with the tide, something so horrible that he was
almost reluctant to use it.

Ho stood with young Major Xuyen from the

213th PAVN. The young officer didn't know the reason Comrade Ho wanted this one man so badly but it was not his place to question. He would obey. Two full companies of his regiment were now at the edge of the marsh waiting for the order before entering it. They didn't like the looks of that place and neither did he. They had never gone into the swamps before; there had never been any reason to. They were inhospitable and definitely uninviting. Even the local bandits avoided them, preferring any other place to the marsh.

Still there was only one man in there and his soldiers were all well trained and well equipped regular army personnel who would do their duty. And when they got close to their prey it would be easier. One man in every squad carried a flare gun which could light up the darkest night for a few moments.

"Are you ready to give the order Comrade Colonel?"

Ho was eager to go after this thing in the swamp. It had haunted his every waking moment and most of his sleeping hours far too long. He would have an end to it this night even if it took the lives of every man in the two companies of soldiers with him. There were some things that went even beyond Party loyalty. This was a thing of the soul which had to be laid to rest once and for all.

"Yes! Give the order. If he is killed they are to bring me the body. I must see it for myself. Is that clearly understood?"

"*Toi hieu biet.*" But the major didn't really understand, although he'd transmitted the order to his company commanders and they in turn to their platoons and squads. The order was given to those with flashlights to turn them on. For half a mile around the edge of the marsh, spears of man-made light lanced a few feet into the dark.

"Tien tra trouc!" At the order the two companies set foot into the shallow tepid waters. Ho went with them, staying with the major and his escort. He knew the danger they were in, and that the thing they hunted was not totally human. He had seen the death it dealt. Two companies of 120 men each were not, to his thinking, too many; in fact they might not be enough. Weapons at the ready, they advanced, trying to keep a semblance of a line as they moved into the sucking waters. Only the beams of the flashlights gave their movements any cohesion. Without the lights they would soon be lost and disoriented with no man knowing where his neighbor was.

Casey found the small animal trail he was looking for. It was less than six inches above water level and just wide enough for a deer to walk. Steadily he moved on, ignoring the line of insects and flies that hovered above the murky waters. Once he saw the flicker of a light far behind him and smiled secretly. "Come on in," he whispered. "The water's fine."

It took him fifteen minutes to reach what he was looking for, a small hummock rising six feet above the swamp. One lonely tree stood there waiting, its branches set another five feet above the mound. That was where he would stay. Looking at his watch he noted that there was still over an hour to wait. It should take the PAVN troops at least that long to reach this spot and when they did it would

take a lifetime for them to get back out. He took
the goatskins from around his neck and draped
them over the tree's branches. Checking the grease
gun he worked the action and leaned back to wait.

From his perch he was above most of the lower
mist that covered the swamp. Looking down
through it he could see that the thin trail he had
followed was now only an inch or so above the
water level and soon that would be gone.

Sweat ran in rivers down Ho's face, his breathing heavy, lungs aching as he tried to keep up with
Xuyen and his men. His feet felt as though they
were encased in hundred pound blocks of slime
from the mud that clung to them at every step.
Major Xuyen kept a constant dialogue going with
his flank elements over the walkie-talkies that each
platoon leader had with him. So far, nothing.
Only the swamp and mud. In spots the water was
reaching thigh level. Fifteen minutes into the
marsh and a call came that a jacket had been
found. They were on the right trail!

Casey could smell salt on the air from the unseen sea. The winds were beginning to turn with
the incoming tide. It was time. The trail he had
taken was now invisible. Nearer now were the
beams of light casting about over the marsh. If
he'd judged right, by now the average depth of the
marsh should be nearly hip high. Taking the goatskins from the tree branch he pulled the stopper
on one and then the other and tossed one on each
side of the mound. A dark fluid began to seep
from the skin bags into the murky liquid of the

marsh. The dark, thick blood of a water buffalo drifted heavily with the slow flow of the current as it swirled softly in with the tide. Small fish tasted the blood and came to inspect the source. Behind them came larger ones and not finding anything there they ate the smaller fish.

From the sea, dark shapes rippled on the surface as they came in with the tide. Sliding over mud banks and through salt marsh grass they snaked their way between the tangled roots of the mangrove trees till the first one sensed the distaste of blood in the water. It turned toward the source, the sudden onset of primal hunger driving it. Behind the first came another, then another, riding in with the tide by twos and threes. Then in tens and twenties they came in from the sea and each tasted the blood and swam faster not wanting to be the last.

Major Xuyen did not like the way the search was progressing. In the last half hour the water had been rising steadily. There was no dry ground to be seen. It took an infinity to cover just a few yards. Men were falling constantly or having to be helped out of sink holes. From the marks on the trunks of trees he knew the water level did not get much higher than a man's waist but it gave him small comfort. He was a dry land soldier not a sailor or a fisherman.

Several times he had looked at Ho thinking to ask the colonel if it would not be better to call off the search, at least until the first light of day. The expression on Ho's face and the touch of fever to his eyes made Xuyen change his mind. He would go on. Better the unknown enemy in the swamp than the vengeance of a superior officer who had the power of life and death over him.

Casey looked down through a thin layer of swirling vapor. He thought he saw something go by his mound. The water rippled, left a small wake, and then the ripple disappeared. Less than a minute later there came another one, then a wave of them gathered around the base of the mound.

To the left Casey saw the glow of a flashlight shine upward. A lonely beacon searched the branches of a tree. Other lights were near him now and he could hear the voices of men talking softly to each other asking directions and swearing at the water and the mud. Pulling the shoulder stock out on the grease gun he flicked off the safety and set the submachine gun on his shoulder. The waters churned beneath him as the beasts tasted the blood, hungering for the meat that should be there. He would give them what they wanted. The nearest lights were less than fifty feet away now. Resting his arm against the limb of the tree to steady his gun, he began to take up the slack on the trigger.

The rapid chatter of the submachine gun broke the night. The nearest light went down as three 9 mm bullets tore the chest out of its bearer. Casey swung the weapon right and left. He hit two more Viets, not killing them but putting them down with bleeding wounds. The rest of the squad dropped low in the water for cover. Only their shoulders and weapons rose above the water as they tried to see where the fire had come from.

A young sergeant thought he saw something in the mist. He could just make out a rise and a tree where a dark shape huddled in its bare branches. He raised his AK-47 to his shoulder and was just about to squeeze the trigger, when suddenly something incredibly heavy took his leg and pulled. His finger let go of the trigger. What???? Then he was gone, his mouth filling with swamp water as the thing holding his leg rolled over once, twice, showing the white of its belly briefly as it twisted the sergeant's leg off at the hip. More blood spread, the scent drawing death to the Viets. The man standing next to the now deceased sergeant froze in horror as his squad leader disappeared. He was just starting to cry out a warning when the water in front of him burst open and jaws wide enough to tear a water buffalo's rear leg off and lined with rows of serrated teeth grabbed his head between them and closed, crushing the skull and tearing open the shoulder to expose the chest cavity and lungs. Then it too gave a rolling twist and hauled its meal under the water.

Phang had done as Casey ordered. He had waited till the Vietnamese were well into the swamp and then his men had moved up on its edge, but none of them had entered the water. That they were not to do. Their job was to wait. If things went as planned most of the killing would be done for them.

Van stood off to the side of Phang. He was strangely silent, his normal bravado and quick banter gone. Even though the men in the marsh were his enemies, they were also of his own race. He didn't like what was going to happen to them.

Phang kept his own council. He knew what Van was feeling. He knew he would have felt the same if it had been his people.

Screams began to come from the swamp. Men trying to fight for their lives fired their weapons at random. Some of the lucky ones were hit by their comrades bullets before the jaws took them.

In his tree Casey shuddered. He had seen death dealt in a thousand different ways, but he had never seen anything to equal this. One of the creatures crawled up onto the hummock and stared at him through double-lidded golden eyes. It raised its head, exposed the white of its maw and gave a long harsh honking cry for food. Casey knew that salt water crocodiles often grew to be over twenty feet in length and weighed over a ton. Right now, along with this one, there were hundreds of them in the waters of the marsh and all of them were hungering for food.

Blind panic hit the Viets. Those with flare guns fired them off to try and illuminate the night and give them a chance to fight the things ripping off their legs and arms. Most wished they hadn't, for now they could see the waters around them red with blood as bodies were being torn in half. The great crocodiles were not just killing, they were in a feeding frenzy, taking one then another of the Viets. Machine gun fire and grenades thrown into the marsh did nothing to stop them as hundreds of the beasts clambered over each other to get at the living flesh. Huge jaws opened above the water line as the crocs threw their heads back to toss and gulp down gobbets of meat.

Cries and screams of terror came from all sides. One by one the flashlights went out as the bearers were pulled underwater by the bloodthirsty crocs. When the last of the hand torches went out, the surviving soldiers were left blind in the dark. With no sense of direction most just went deeper into the swamp. Some tried to climb the slick trunks of the mangrove trees only to feel their legs crushed between razor-lined jaws as they were dragged back down.

Phang's men listened to the screams of the dying with mixed emotions. There were feelings of exultation that their hated enemy was being destroyed and those of revulsion at their grisly deaths. War was war but there was something to be said about being eaten alive by reptiles that even their toughened hides couldn't bear. Van said nothing, the tears running down his boyish face evidence enough of his anguish.

Phang wondered how his long nosed friend was faring inside that watery place of death.

Casey sat still in his tree, stunned and in a state of half-shock at that which he had wrought. The huge reptiles were piled on top of each other snapping and gulping down the torn pieces of flesh that had once been living men. The grunts and groans of the hundreds of sea crocs in their feeding frenzy was a form of madness he had never expected to let loose upon the world.

CHAPTER NINETEEN

Colonel Ho screamed in panic as the waters around him erupted with monstrous feeding reptiles. One was coming straight for him. He pulled his pistol and fired three rounds straight at the head. The slugs from the Tokarev didn't even phase the monster; it came on. Xuyen tried to break and run but his feet were held fast in the sucking bottom. Ho moved behind him. The croc was nearly on them. Xuyen reached out his hand to Ho for help, but the colonel shot him between the eyes, pushed the body in front of him and moved away. The sea croc took Xuyen between his jaws and sank beneath the water. A small enough sacrifice for your leader, Xuyen.

Ho stopped trying to fight his way by wading. His boots had already been torn off by the sludge so he lay face down in the water and began to half swim, half crawl his way out of the swamp. By now the horrible cries of dying men were beginning to fade.

Ho bumped into several bodies in his flight to escape the reptiles. None of them had all of their parts. Some were torn in two; others had no arms, legs or heads. He yelled at one man whose upper body blocked his passage. The man didn't respond. Ho pushed at his shoulders. The upper torso leaned over to sink head down. He had been torn in half, the air in the upper chest cavity keeping the corpse afloat.

Fearful of looking behind him, Ho kept his eyes to the front. Every shadow or swirl of water caused his heart to pound in terror.

As he moved away from the place of slaughter, lone survivors tried to join him. Recognizing him as an officer, they wanted someone, anyone to tell them what to do. He moved away from them, fearful that the sounds of too many men would draw more of the crocs to them. Ho went on alone veering off to the right. He reached out to push a half-submerged log out of the way when it whipped around and looked at him. The hinged upper jaw opening. Ho couldn't even scream. His bowels let loose draining down the inside of his pants leg and he didn't even know it. Somewhere he found strength he didn't know he had. Grabbing the base of the nearest tree, he used the broken trunk of the mangrove to get him out of the water and high enough so he could shimmy up the slick trunk into the nearest branches. The croc below him was not one of the huge creatures who had destroyed the two companies of the 213th Regiment. It was a baby weighing in at only three or four hundred pounds.

Ho was not going to go any further this night. He had found a refuge and there he would stay; let the others do what they wanted. Here he was safe. As for the rest of the two companies, there weren't too many who had made it away from the crocodiles. Of the over two hundred men who had gone into the marsh less than fifteen made it within sight of land.

• • •

Straining his eyes, Phang tried to see into the mist and beyond the first line of swamp grass. His men looked at each other as they listened to their enemies die. Most made signs to ward off evil or touched amulets to protect themselves from the spirits of those who were dying. The Kamserai were not men who were noted for their deep altruistic feelings, but this manner of death had something that felt unclean about it.

Phang was of the same stock. He too touched his amulet, prepared by a powerful shaman. It was made of secret things which would protect him from the unseen and keep unfriendly spirits at bay. Phang could read and write. He had been to the big cities of Phnom Penh and Saigon. He knew of penicillin and of television. He was not an ignorant savage. Like most tribesmen who had been raised in an animistic society, he feared nothing that he could touch or see, but no matter what else he had been exposed to in the outside world he still believed in the spirits of the dead and their ability to do good and evil to the living. He found no contradiction in this. Did not the Catholics believe that their invisible god could touch them and do good and evil?

Van heard them coming, the cries of fear and the whimpering of grown men, the sloshing of weary feet in the water. He almost hated to do what he had to do. They had been through a nightmare that no man could ever imagine, unless he were mad. Van took the safety off his weapon. He would do what he had to. . . .

They were to hold their fire till he was sure that

most of the Viets were all together or they were spotted.

One by one the VC began to emerge from the dark, deadly waters. No man helped another. Each was driven by his personal instinct for survival. Once out of the marsh they collapsed, trying to breathe as they fought to control the shaking of their limbs.

Phang waited a few moments more till a *Chung uy* from the 213th stood up and looked around him. He saw the lieutenant from the 213th lock on the face of Van looking back at him from a distance of no more than twenty feet. The exhausted lieutenant was glad to see anyone who might help. He reached out his hands in supplication. Van raised the Savage 12 gauge automatic shotgun and put a solid slug through the lieutenant's mouth taking the back of the man's head off. When he fired, Phang gave the order to the rest of his men. They opened up with all they had. It was a relief for them to kill something themselves rather than leave everything to the swamp. Machine gun and rifle fire poured down on the few survivors. Some of them could have escaped Phang's ambush by going back into the marsh, but not one man did that. All chose to stay where they were and take the easy way out. Phang rationalized that at least their death was easier this way than in the marsh. He went to check the bodies, putting single pistol shots into each man's skull. It was always best to make sure.

Phang wondered again about his scar-faced friend with the gray-blue eyes, whose soul had such a feeling of desolation about it that just being around the man sometimes made him feel as if eternity's breath had touched him for just a moment. What was this man doing now in the marsh, where so many were dying?

Casey stayed in his tree as he must till the tide turned again. The firing from the edge of the marsh was less than he'd expected. Phang must not have had to work as hard as he thought he would. The sounds of feeding had abated now. The crocs' voracious appetites were sated. Some took cadavers with them to bury in secret places in the mud, till they ripened enough to please the reptiles' palates. Several times, one or another of the monsters would crawl up to the base of his tree and look at him with its golden eyes, but they left him alone. The tree was his sanctuary.

Casey never slept in the safety of his tree. His mind stayed in a kind of half-daze that let the remaining hours till dawn pass without notice. The tide had gone back out and with it most of the crocodiles. There were probably a few left behind who preferred to wallow in the deep pools of cool mud, or sleep in their burrows after a heavy meal.

The trail was again visible when he slid down the tree to stand on the mound. His body ached; every muscle in his limbs creaked and cracked. Stretching them out to loosen up, he breathed deep and looked around him. All was quiet.

Taking the trail as far as he could before going back into the waters, his stomach churned. Several times he wanted to throw up, and would have if there'd been anything inside him. Scattered about were the signs of last night's reptilian bacchanalia. Scraps of uniforms floated here and there, and at times he saw pieces of meat floating loose on the surface. An entire arm, still wearing a khaki sleeve, moved gently in the water, vibrating and jerking as fish and crabs competing with each other tugged at it. The crocs were gone but the blue marsh crabs were everywhere. Thousands of them. It was a normal thing in nature's scheme. After the big creatures fed, the smaller ones cleaned up the mess. He kicked them off the trail with his bare feet, ignoring the clacking pincers.

By the time he reached the edge of the swamp and had stepped over the bodies of the dead Charlies Phang had killed, the heat of the morning had burned off the last of the mist, leaving the marsh quiet and serene—a completely different picture than the one of the previous night. Herons and waterfowl came as they always did to nest and feed. Flowers opened bright petals to the sun. He looked back at the still waters and shuddered.

Phang came to him, his dark face filled with concern:

"It was a bad thing to see, was it not, my friend?"

Casey nodded. "Yes, it was a very bad thing. I don't believe I could do it again."

Van stood silent, his shotgun lowered to the earth. Casey went to him. "It's over now. We'll leave soon."

Walking back to the bodies he looked them over. Ho wasn't among them. He shrugged, too tired to worry about it. Either Ho had been taken by the crocs or he was still alive. Right now it made no difference. He just wanted to get away from there. Most likely his protagonist was firmly settled in the belly of one or more of the sea crocs.

Still he had a feeling that his mission was not yet over. Not until he had either hard confirmation from intelligence sources that Ho was dead or he saw the body himself. If Ho was among those taken by the crocs he'd find out sooner or later. He hoped that the enemy colonel was dead. He was growing very weary of this game of hide and kill.

Ho couldn't leave the marsh. The small crocodile had settled down on a mud bank to rest in the sun. Every time Ho made a move one of its eyes would blink and Ho would freeze. He wasn't going any place until the beast left.

Casey replaced his missing boots with a pair of rubber sandals made from the tire off a ¾ ton truck. Phang gave his men orders to strip all the bodies and bring any papers they had on them to him. He would translate them later. Right now, he like everyone else, wanted to be away from this unclean place.

Forming in a single file with flankers out, the Kamserai and the scar-faced man with Van behind him headed back to the north, to where they belonged. All that day they marched in silence, each man left to his own thoughts. Casey stayed in the middle of the column. It felt somehow reassuring to have men in front and in back of him, living men.

They passed through two villages that day where women prepared food and cared for their babies while their men worked the small fields outside the hamlet, as they always had. They looked at Casey with curiosity, for many of them had never seen a white man in person and, if they all looked like this one, then they did not wish to see another one. When they asked what had happened, the Kamserai said nothing. They only shook their heads and moved on. This was not the time for the telling of tales. Later, when the memory had a chance to fade and the horror was a bit less real, they would then tell the story of the night of the crocodiles. It would be told and retold around the campfires of their longhouses, and with each telling the story would grow and so would the fear that only a legend with the taste of truth brings with it. In centuries yet to come, the salt marsh would be avoided at all costs, and if one heard the harsh, honking cry of a crocodile he might have a momentary vision of hundreds of men being devoured by the largest of the world's living reptiles.

CHAPTER TWENTY

Near the outskirts of Kompot, Casey suddenly called a halt. Phang went to him. "What is it? Why do we stop? Have you seen something?

Casey shook his head. "No! It's not what I've seen. It's what I have not seen that bothers me. I'm going back to the marsh. I've got to know if Ho is still alive. I grow very weary of this game and wish to see an end to it. If he is alive in the swamp, I'll find him. If he is dead, then I'll know that too. Anyway, the answers are back there."

Phang started to order his men to turn around to head back, but Casey stopped him. "No! This is one thing I need to do by myself. You and your men make camp here. If I'm not back by dawn, two days from now, go on to your homes and I'll catch up with you later."

Phang would have preferred to return with his friend, for the swamp had always been a place of evil and one should not go there alone.

Casey knew what Phang was thinking. "Trust me, Old One. I'll return. I always do and always will." Phang felt there was a certain truth in the words, but he could not say why. But he believed. And that was sufficient. "As you wish Big Nose. We will wait till the dawn, two days from now."

Van was still in a kind of soul shock. When Casey said he was going back he half stumbled as he turned back the way they had come. He was stopped by a firm but gentle hand on his shoulder.

"No! This is not for you. I want you to stay with Phang till I get back." Van looked up at him with sad brown eyes that told of his inner torment. He nodded his head in acceptance of his friend's order. He would go with the Kamserai and wait.

Casey faced back to the sea. He would have to hurry if he wanted to get there before nightfall, and he did. Settling into a mile eating half trot, he went back the way he had come. One mile after another he ran, letting his mind detach itself from his body as the miles passed behind him. He had to find out. He knew that if he waited he would know in time, but he didn't want to wait any longer. This had gone on too long and it was time for it to be finished. If Ho was in the swamp alive, he'd find him.

From his perch, Ho watched the crocodile. His arms and legs trembled from the strain of remaining in one spot so long. He moved a leg and wiggled the foot to get the circulation flowing again. When he did the croc blinked once and Ho was still again. Even though he knew the beast couldn't get to him in the tree he didn't want to draw anymore attention from it than necessary. If he stayed up there long enough perhaps the beast would lose interest and go after an easier meal. As the sun came and went overhead, and the heat of the day grew greater, the crocodile moved back into the water and lowered his body to where just the large golden eyes showed above the surface.

Ho was miserable. Flies and mosquitoes picked at his flesh, sucking his blood and leaving itches that couldn't be scratched. Thirst and worry turned his mouth slimy and foul tasting. All of his misery he credited to the damned one who should have died long ago but still stayed to haunt his every hour. Was he a *Thay phu*, a wizard with powers outside those of normal men, or was he a *Tao vat xe Hou nguc*, a creature from hell? Ho had long thought himself to be too sophisticated and well educated to believe in witchcraft and devils, but of late his mind had turned more frequently to those stories told in the villages by old men and women, stories of demons that walked the earth in human form and brought misfortune. Surely, he had been given over to the forces of evil, for his luck had gone from bad to worse. He looked down from his safe limb. Where was the *Con cu sau*? It had disappeared. He looked hard at the water. From this height he should have been able to see the body of the croc, even under water. It was nowhere in sight. He twisted around the tree trunk and looked as far as his eyes could see, checking every patch of swamp grass, every mound of mud where the beast could have gone. It wasn't to be seen. Perhaps it had given up, as he had hoped it would, and had gone to seek another meal. He waited a bit longer. The lengthening of the shadows said that another night was on the way and, if he was going to leave, it would have to be now. The idea of spending one more night in this place of death gave him the courage to crawl down from his limb and place his feet back into the water. It was still shallow; the tide hadn't begun to come in yet. If he hurried he could be out of the swamp before it did, bringing back with it the dreaded crocodiles.

His only weapon was his pistol, and that he kept in his hand, the hammer cocked and ready to fire. One step at a time he moved, afraid to go too fast because of the noise it would make and the creatures it might attract. Every shadow was a terror. Every jumping fish made his heart leap into his throat and nearly choke him.

At last he could no longer restrain himself. The shadows were growing too long and the dark was going to be coming very soon to the swamp. He moved faster, more confident that he had a chance to get out alive. If he did, he would go so deep in the jungles that no one would ever hear from him again. He'd had enough of everything. His confidence was broken and the ideologies that he'd believed in and had been ready to die for no longer seemed of any importance. They were only shallow things that had served to give him the feeling of a mission in life, something to live for. Now he had another mission, and that was simply to live.

Through a break in the trees he saw a rise in the land, a hill that was not part of the marsh. Tears of relief came to his eyes. He sobbed with joy! He was going to make it! He was going to be all right. He had survived. Any thought or concern for the nearly two hundred men who had died in the marsh for him never entered his mind. He was going to live; that was all that was important. He was going to get away. Splashing his way now, he tore at the swamp, forcing his legs to go as fast as they could through the sucking mud. He ignored the whipping lashes of branches and vines that cut his face and tore his uniform. The pain was nothing. He was going to *live!*

Ho reached the first patch of solid ground. Beyond it he could see there was no more water. He was out! He fell to the earth, grateful, sucking in great gasps of breath to feed his oxygen starved system. Every muscle and nerve in his body trembled with relief and exhaustion. Sobbing, he gave thanks to the spirits of his fathers for his salvation.

A shadow fell over him. A sudden chill started deep in the pit of his stomach. He raised his face from the safe, good earth.

Casey stood on a small rise, the sun behind him. He watched Ho as he struggled to his feet on weak, shaking legs.

Eyes wide with shock, Ho pointed his finger at Casey. His words came out thin and ragged. "*Qui than!* Demon!" Casey stood silent. Only his eyes moved as he watched Ho. He knew the man was on the razor's edge of madness, needing only a small push to send him over.

Ho began to raise his pistol. The Tokarev felt as though it had weights tied to it. His arm barely had the strength to get the pistol up to shoulder level. His arm and hand trembled with the strain. Tears came to his eyes as he cried out again, "*Qui than!*"

Casey thought that perhaps Ho was closer to the truth than even he knew. If there were demons to be found on the face of the earth, surely he had to qualify as being one.

The Tokarev pointed in his direction and still he didn't move. Ho's entire body was shaking as he mustered the strength to pull the trigger. The bullet passed over three feet away from its target. Ho groaned and fired again. The shaking of his body was so bad that he couldn't have hit a tank at ten feet. "Die!" he screamed. "Why don't you die and leave me alone?"

Casey shook his head almost sadly as he answered. "I would die if I could." Ho didn't hear him. He tried to fire again but the magazine was empty. He dropped the weapon. Madness was on him, riding his soul like a dark wind.

He choked out, "I know that you have come to steal my soul. But you can't have it. I won't let you."

Tears streaming from his eyes, he turned blindly and ran back into the marsh, laughing insanely, repeating over and over to the wind and sky, "You can't have me. . . ."

Casey didn't follow. When he saw that Ho was mad, he knew the chase was over. He no longer wanted to kill him. Something much worse had already taken his prey from him.

Ho stumbled, crawled, and beat his way back into the darkening marsh. His eyes sightless, he saw nothing. He ran till the heavy shadows of night sat on the waters. The very fabric of his mind had ripped. He didn't even see the golden eyes directly in front of him, or the gaping maw that rushed to meet him. Only when the jaws closed on his leg to drag him under did he scream, and then it was because he thought the demon had taken him. He tried to scream again, but it was stopped when pointed teeth severed his head from his body.

Casey heard the death cry and shuddered. He

knew what had happened and how Ho had died.

"The fool should have let me kill him. It would have been much better. . . ."

There was nothing left for him here; he could go back now.

Phang wondered how his friend had fared in his quest. That he would return was never Phang's doubt. Still, he and Van, who had begun by now to return to the real world, stayed awake all that long night and waited. It was only when the cooking fires of the morning were lit and rice was being prepared that a hail from one of the Kamserai sentries brought them to their feet. Casey was back. Van and Phang rushed to meet their friend. From the expression in the gray-blue eyes both men knew the long hunt was over.

Casey said nothing, only nodded his greetings and went to a grassy spot under a tree and lay down. Taking one deep breath he closed his eyes and went to sleep. He was very, very tired.

Phang squatted on his haunches to wait till Casey awoke, then he would have the last of the story. When Casey lay down to rest so did Van. Both men needed the healing powers of sleep.

It was the next morning before Casey stirred from his deep slumber. He told Phang and Van of Ho's death and the Kamserai touched his bag of charms. "My friend, it is time for you to leave and go back to your own kind."

Casey smiled grimly and thought, *My own kind? There is none that I can call my own kind.*

The column formed up and they moved out. Phang would provide an escort for him and Van back to South Vietnam.

For the next three days they moved steadily on, recrossing the same fields and rivers until they reached the flat rice lands of the upper delta, near Ha Tien. That night they rested only a few miles from an American outpost. They would wait till full light before going in. That way there would be little chance that they'd be mistaken for Vietcong.

When they neared the outskirts of Ha Tien they encountered a small fortified guard post where fifty ARVIN and a dozen American soldiers guarded the western approach to the city. At a distance of seven hundred meters from the main gate, Phang said his farewells. He had no need to go any further and two men would not be as likely to excite a trigger happy soldier as would his band which, from a distance looked much the same as any other band of guerrillas or bandits.

He held Casey's arm and squeezed. "Live long and well, my friend. If ever you have need of me you have but to call and I will answer. As long as there is life in my body and strength in my limbs I will come. Live long! Live well!" To Van there was little that could be said. They merely smiled at each other and that was the end of it. There was no need for words.

Casey returned the squeeze and hugged the old barbarian around the shoulders before turning his back. With Van at his side, he walked toward the outpost. Phang and his men faded away, back into high grass. They turned back to their homelands in Cambodia, where their wives and children awaited their return.

A sentry on the main gate called out to the sergeant of the guard. "Hey, Sarge, there's someone coming in. There's two of them. One of them looks like a GI. He's too damned big to be a gook.''

SFC Lansing climbed on top of the sandbagged wall and looked out. "You're right, it is an American. Take a couple of men and go out and bring him in. But watch the Viet with him. It might be a trap of some kind."

The sentry took two PFCs with him, opened the main gate under the protective sights of an M-60 light machine gun, and went out. They were about four hundred meters from the main gate when they met.

Casey raised a hand in greeting as the corporal began to question him about what the hell he was doing out in the boondocks with just a single Viet for company. The questioning was abruptly stopped when the corporal disappeared in an exploding cloud. Casey felt a hammer blow hit his head and then darkness took him. He wasn't aware of the rest of the half dozen 81 mm mortar rounds that came in around them. A Vietcong mortar crew had snuck in close during the night and was laying down a few rounds of harassing fire. After they got off their six rounds they grabbed their tube and ran for it. Unfortunately, they ran right into Phang, who was pleased to acquire such a valuable addition to his armory.

The two surviving privates covered Van as he somehow hoisted the larger man onto his shoulders and hauled Casey across the field into the gates of the outpost. The two privates decided quickly that there wasn't any sense in trying to bring in the corporal. There wasn't enough of him left to make an armful. Besides which they hadn't liked him very much anyway.

Van stayed with Casey as a medic checked him over. The medic had seen many wounds before but was amazed that the guy with the scar was still alive, even though part of his skull was blown open.

Casey had not yet awakened when the dust-off chopper came in for him. Van had to remain behind as the chopper took his friend away. The dust-off had a full load of other wounded aboard and there just wasn't room for him. He waved his farewell to the chopper as it disappeared.

Instead of taking their brain-injured casualty to Saigon, the chopper pilot put the machine balls to the wall and headed for Nha Trang. The other wounded were not in serious shape so the scar-faced man had first priority. The outpost medic had radioed the hospital at Ton son Nhut and had been told that the best neurosurgeon in Nam was in Nha Trang right now, and that was where they were to deliver their casualty. To the 8th Field Hospital at Nha Trang . . .

EPILOGUE

Well, my dear Landries, that is how Casey Romain came to us at the 8th Field Hospital. The rest you know as well as I. If your memory is rusty on any of the fine points, I refer you to your copy of *Casca: The Eternal Mercenary*.

Till next time,
Julius Goldman, M.D.